THE LEGACY SERIES

Series Titles

Sometimes Creek
Steve Fox

Where Are Your People From?
James B. De Monte

Self-Defense
Corey Mertes

Finding the Bones: Stories & A Novella
Nikki Kallio

The Plagues
Joe Baumann

The Clayfields
Elise Gregory

Kind of Blue
Christopher Chambers

Evangelina Everyday
Dawn Burns

Township
Jamie Lyn Smith

Responsible Adults
Patricia Ann McNair

Great Escapes from Detroit
Joseph O'Malley

Nothing to Lose
Kim Suhr

The Appointed Hour
Susanne Davis

Praise for
Sometimes Creek

"Perfectly Midwestern, perfect portraits of perfectly imperfect people. Like coal that never turns into diamonds, but sparks up just the same."

—Amber Sparks
author of *And I Do Not Forgive You*

"*Sometimes Creek* is unlike any collection of stories I've read in a long time. What delights most about these stories is their tough and sweet humanity, stories of people with troubled souls: the grief-stricken, the unmoored. The world of this book is our world, familiar and confounding, seen through a cracked and colorful glass. Endlessly surprising, strange, and satisfying. Steve Fox writes with clarity about his characters and the places they live. He loves them, and so you will remember and hold them dear after you close the book."

—Richard Mirabella
author of *Brother & Sister Enter the Forest*

"Somehow Steve Fox has fused together the gravity, emotion, and darkness of William Gay, Tim O'Brien, and Ron Rash. You fall into these words, are enveloped by these lives, troubled by the uncanny—coming away from this collection moved, haunted, and not quite intact."

—Richard Thomas
author of *Spontaneous Human Combustion*

"*Sometimes Creek* is a surefooted debut centered on the myriad tender, complicated ways we connect with one another. Fox carefully tilts the familiar until it shimmers—these are stories of real life in all its strange wonder and quiet magic."

—Kimberly King Parsons
author of *Black Light*
National Book Award Finalist

"This is astonishingly good storytelling by Steve Fox. With an assured, direct narrative voice and deep understanding of human nature, Fox spins stories with deliciously dark underbellies, stories that leave the reader satisfied and just a touch unsettled. The Midwestern landscape of Fox's imagining is the stubbled field in late November variety, with a twisted, grinning scarecrow at its center. By turns moving and funny and gothic, and always compelling, *Sometimes Creek* is a collection to savor."

—Kathy Fish
author of *Wild Life: Collected Works*

"Don't be fooled. Disturbing themes hide behind Midwestern idioms and friendly banter in Steve Fox's arresting *Sometimes Creek*. With a keen eye to the darker side of human existence, Fox explores the uneasy relationships we have with nature, with pets, with people, with the ones we love. Some of these marvelous stories sparkle with magical realism and others gut punch with frank reality. All together, this is one dazzling collection you'll start to read and won't want to put down."

—Alice Kaltman
author of *Almost Deadly, Almost Good* and *Dawg Towne*

"In this heartfelt debut collection, readers immediately know where they are: in Steve Fox's America. Hardscrabble and tender, these seventeen story gems gleam in Midwestern dust. These are tales of joy, loss, winning, losing and persevering; infused with Fox's wry humor at just the right moments. The word that stands out most is serendipity, in a collection that surprises in all the best ways. Guided by Fox's skillful pen, take a journey to *serendipity—Sometimes Creek*, always memorable."

—Amy Cipolla Barnes
author of *Mother Figures, Ambrotypes*, and *Child Craft*

"I've been following Steve Fox's short stories for several years now, and he never disappoints. It's downhome literary fiction. These are beautifully crafted pieces of art, but you don't notice that at first – you notice characters that feel real within the first page of the story, settings that remind you of home (wherever you grew up), and the often odd, even macabre, events happening in the middle of a Norman Rockwell painting. All written in such a way that I would occasionally reread a sentence just to wallow in the light-touch simple beauty of his prose. Each is truly a gem."

—Robb Grindstaff
author of *June Bug Gothic: Tales from the South* and *Slade*
Pinnacle Book Achievement Award Winner

"In this rich, eclectic collection, Steve Fox captures the hard-scrabble life of Midwestern folk, mixes in gothic elements and magical realism, and provides glimpses of the hopes and hurts in the human heart. Each story envelops the reader in its unique world peopled with characters that are at once mystical and real. Reminiscent of stories by T.C. Boyle and George Saunders, Fox's work resonates with the reader long after the final page has been turned."

—Kim Suhr
author of *Nothing to Lose*

"Steve Fox writes with a voice that pounds a stake in the ground, claiming a literary territory all his own. These stories will rattle the cages of your day-to-day state of mind. This collection is akin to veering off of the familiar highway, down a road you've never seen, then stomping on the accelerator. Expect to be surprised, elated, and crushed. Hold on to the wheel and take this ride wide-eyed."

—William Burtch
co-author of *W.G.*

"Steve Fox's writerly antenna pulls in powerful 50,000-watt transmissions from quiet Midwestern lives. Haunted and unsettling, but somehow normal, *Sometimes Creek* is a virtuoso necromancy of people turned inside out and then folded back to a reality that we somehow recognize. Fox's world, gently strange and skewed on the page, is a place of deeply human truth and beauty."

—Barry Wightman
author of *Pepperland*
President, Wisconsin Writers Association

"The stories in Steve Fox's collection, *Sometimes Creek*, manage the feat of being both entertaining and enlightening. His agile prose conjures portals that allow the reader to effortlessly slide deep into the psyche of his characters, as they navigate through their always interesting, and sometimes strange, situations. Whether real or surreal, Fox's enjoyable tales prompt us to examine our own values and behaviors, while having a little fun along the way."

—Michael Hopkins
contributor, *Coolest American Stories*

"Reading this collection is like falling into a Magritte painting and finding that hey, some of these people are pretty nice. To varying degrees, these pieces embrace the surreal, the dark, the weird; but there's a tenderness to the way the stories treat their characters. Unfulfilled longing runs through most of the collection; many of the stories feature protagonists in the throes of an incomplete understanding of the losses they've suffered. Fox sets his stories in old neighborhoods in small Midwestern towns that are both disturbing and comforting, alien and familiar. And ultimately your heart goes out to this neighborly parade of characters confronting the absurdity of loss."

—Tim Storm
founder of Storm Writing School

"The world inside Steve Fox's brilliant debut collection, *Sometimes Creek*, teeters at the furthest edges of plausibility while remaining open to the subtlest imparts of magic. Like a magnet tugging at these stories, these characters, we too conduct Fox's masterly constructions of tension and strangeness, familiar but destabilized, often culminating in the unforgettable—moments that can frighten and confound as often as they move. To enter any one of these seventeen stories is to experience the feeling of both return and discovery, of coming back to a place you've never actually been. Steve Fox is one of my favorite writers writing fiction today. This collection is a stunner."

—David Byron Queen
word west press

October 2023 . Waukesha -

SOMETIMES CREEK

for Jacki -

Honored to put
this book into your hands.

Stories by

STEVE FOX

Enjoy.

Cornerstone Press
Stevens Point, Wisconsin

Cornerstone Press, Stevens Point, Wisconsin 54481
Copyright © 2023 Steve Fox
www.uwsp.edu/cornerstone

Printed in the United States of America by
Point Print and Design Studio, Stevens Point, Wisconsin

Library of Congress Control Number: 2022944333
ISBN: 979-8-9861447-6-4

Cornerstone Press titles are produced in courses and internships offered by the
Department of English at the University of Wisconsin–Stevens Point.

DIRECTOR & PUBLISHER   EXECUTIVE EDITOR
Dr. Ross K. Tangedal   Jeff Snowbarger

SENIOR EDITORS
Lexie Neeley, Monica Swinick, Kala Buttke

PRESS STAFF
Alyssa Bronk, Grace Dahl, Patrick Fogarty, Angela Green, Cal Henkens, Brett Hill,
Ryan Jensen, Julia Kaufman, Hunter Kiesow, Adam King, Amanda Leibham, Maria
Scherer, Abbi Wasielewski

For Larry

Stories

Exile   1

Randy Koenig's Very Large Mouse   25

Larmet Lunker   35

little blind flying mice   43

Boydlehook   61

The Butcher's Ghost   63

Yard Mary   75

Oliebollen Destiny   91

Everyone Is Dead   109

Goat Milk   125

Unresolved   133

Orange Tree Dog   141

I Prefer You in Spanish   157

Dumplings   169

You're Soaking In It   173

Then It Would Be Raining   185

Sometimes Creek   203

Acknowledgments   221

Exile

Practice is over. You've planted your butt firmly upon the wooden bench of the warming hut, where your stiff fingers unlace hockey skates covered in fresh ice shavings. Around you, other boys revel in the glory and agony of tonight's scrimmage, still breathing hard. Your side lost, and it's very possible it was your fault. But then again, it's always your fault.

What did you do this time? With less than a minute to play, and the score knotted at two, you carried the puck over the other side's blue line into the attacking zone, skillfully drawing both defenders to you inside the left face-off circle. It was a perfect move. The thuggish defenders closed upon you eagerly, leaving Eddie Farrar wide open in the slot mere yards in front of the opposing side's net, ready to score the game-winning goal. He rapped the ice with his stick. Your eyes met. And in a forever instant of that eternal moment, you decided against it. Called the whole thing off. The pass to Eddie Farrar that everyone saw coming. His shot tearing into the mesh at the back of the net.

You'd already done the hard part by sucking both defenders away from the center iceman, Eddie. All you had to do was pass the puck to him. And the enormous and skilled Eddie Farrar, who sports a blinding wrist-shot and who never misses, would have scored, and your side would have emerged the victor. Eddie was *wide open* and yet you,

1

normally the team player, chose not to pass the puck to him. End of story.

Almost. You know better. You still have another skate to pull off and a duffel to pack and you have no idea if your dad's going to show up on time to pick you up on this frigid night. Plus you will very soon have substantial flak to deflect from Eddie and his a-hole sidekicks before your punctualphobic father finally arrives.

So, yeah. Eddie would have scored. He was *wide open*. And you can't believe Diekert hasn't reamed you for it yet.

Actually, you can. That's because Coach Diekert, right on schedule, is still outside pulling on his post-practice smoke and brandy-filled flask with one of the other coaches. They don't think you guys know.

Your hands and feet ache from the cold. You press your fingertips together and ball your hands into tight fists and open them slowly above an old electric heater, coated in a leprosy of rust, rattling away in the corner. You're surprised it still works. Local lore has it that generations of boys have survived dares to piss on the thing in order to prove or (hopefully) disprove the theory that you can electrocute yourself, brutally, in the dick by way of a stream of urine. So far as you can tell, though, the stories of the random sap jolted backwards onto his ass, rendered unconscious and partially naked may be just that—stories. Yet there's no denying what this source of heat smells like.

Your name is Arthur Penske and you are ten-and-a-half years old and you like words—a lot. Like the shape, sound, meaning, and power of words. How they feel when you roll them around in your mouth, curl them with your tongue, when they part your teeth and lips. Already your dictionary at home is all marked up—endless pages of words starred and underlined and highlighted. When you look up a word's definition, you spend several minutes more reading definitions above and below the one you were looking up in the first place. It's only a matter of time until you stumble upon, with tremendous satisfaction, *serendipity.*

This word-fetish trait of yours makes the other boys on your team want to check you into the boards even harder. You don't know why. But you've mastered the Reverse Harpoon. It's a deft method of your own invention for defending yourself against the guys you're not fast enough to skate away from. At the very last possible second, you slide your top hand down your hockey stick ever so slightly when they try to board you from behind. When they hit you—and, there is no "if" in this scenario . . . they *will* hit you, hard—from behind, they jam the butt of your stick, the blade of which you have pressed firmly into the base of the boards, deep into the guts of their solar plexus. And, once harpooned, always shy. Well, shy at least until the pain wears off and their feeble little goldfish brains forget, and they come at you again five or so minutes later.

But they're a-holes anyway, and you've learned this much about them: They are forever doomed to be just that. Except for Eddie Farrar, unfortunately. His parents are really nice, so your mom and dad logically conclude there may one day be hope for him, too. But not you. You have absolutely no trouble envisioning Eddie's now super-nice father as a once-eleven-year-old dickhead. This is because you're still dealing with a fresh, steaming serving of present-day Eddie, who remains an a-hole and continues to behave exactly like one during this current version of your present. And you'd like to treat him like the giant a-hole he is, too. But he's too big. So you need to resort to petty behavior in order to get back at him.

You hear a tittering at the mention of an object that measures eleven and a half inches in length. You haven't started to mature yet, you're reminded yet again, though some of these boys . . . But then you hear they're talking about Mr. Davidson—Phil's dad—who ran off to the clinic last Fourth of July with what he thought had been an embedded deer tick below his earlobe which instead turned out to be a massive ingrown hair. The doctor pulled the coiled mass slowly with a pair of tweezers, revealing inch by inch, an ever-lengthening black thread of horror and pus.

"Hey Pensk," a friendly voice says. A thrill surges through you as you realize the voice comes from one of the cooler kids on the team. The next-best player on the team, in fact, who now calls out your name how you'd like the guys to call you: Pensk.

"Sup, Hutch?" you ask, looking up from your skate, acting as though Brent Hutchinson is always asking you stuff, wondering what you think of this or that, or always just b.s.ing with you about anything, just because. You smile nonchalantly, and give a stock shrug, wiping down the blade of a skate with a cloth. Normal stuff for you and Hutch, this.

"Dickish move out there," he sneers, and nods in Eddie's direction. "Shoulda passed the g-", he says, and your ears go blind as he takes the Lord's name in vain so as to condemn to eternal flames a small, black, rubberized object. A hockey puck.

"An be a f-"— Chris Willems, one of Eddie's lackeys blurts, inserting the f-word descriptor, adding the '-ing' adjectival ending—"team player!" He folds his arms and sneers, as if he'd been waiting all night to say: "Ain't no 'I' in team, *Pinky!*" He grins at Eddie and Hutch obediently.

Your ears are still ringing yet you can hear them titter. But only for another moment as they abruptly fall silent, snapping their heads around, wary and ever vigilant for Coach Diekert. They never speak like this, never repeat the language Diekert berates you guys with, when Diekert himself is around. But he's likely still outside pulling on his flask or second smoke or both. Your coach, who finds himself ever so clever, pumping his throat muscles on the other end of a shiny flask he slips into a breast pocket while you guys buzz around that rink, a jar full of hollering yellow-jackets.

You don't know what to say. What can you say? You should have passed the puck. Everyone in the entire county knows this. And if they don't, well, it'll be all over school tomorrow: Instead of trying to stick-handle your way through two defenders and get the puck stolen for a critical turn-over that led to a two-on-one break-away and the decisive goal for the other team with mere seconds remaining to play—it doesn't matter if your goalie is a total sieve and should have stopped that lame back-handed deke in the first place—you should have passed the puck to Eddie when you so artfully drew both defenders to you, leaving Eddie with his powerful wrist-shot *completely alone* in front of the net.

But Eddie is an a-hole. A big enough a-hole to compel you to risk the outcome of the game. Anything, really, to deny Eddie yet more certain glory you'd never, ever, hear the end of. You shove your other skate and helmet into your *not-gay!*-brother's duffel and stand up to leave. You don't need a reason. He's an a-hole. That's your story and you're sticking to it.

Outside, the boys await parents, stamping feet. Moms and dads roll into the parking lot near the rink, rounding the high school building in their large new cars, always shiny no matter the season—early winter, mid-winter, late-winter, or next winter—marching forward, dutifully in procession, a tight stream of carpenter ants on parade, to gather their children, one gleaming new vehicle at a time.

Hardening molasses minutes pass. Dad doesn't come. It's just you and Devon now. Devon is mostly your physical and social equal, and for a moment you allow your guard to slip. But tonight even Devon can't resist the contagion of Eddie's a-holiness. He starts in on you, Pinky. Pinky the wall-crawler, the boy who wishes himself into invisibility each time he steps into the school building. The one who packs slices of dread into his cold lunch every morning. The kid who brings upon himself an isolation of despair.

You're good at ignoring your near-equal peers, though, and your eyes slide away from him and lock onto the spot where your dad's car should be rounding the corner of the building. And just as you start to drift away from Devon, his mom suddenly barrels around the corner in her black Volvo sedan, the exaggerated speed an apology for her tardiness. Always flustered, Devon's very pretty mother normally says something, breathless, about being so terribly, terribly busy. There's a roar and a bounce of headlights off Devon's eyes. He flashes you a threatening glance, shakes his head, and climbs into the back seat of his mom's car, fully domesticated and reduced to a sweet little boy again. Just another tough guy whose turn it probably is to do the dishes.

Your dad is still nowhere in sight. You're relieved. Freezing, but relieved. Relieved because you don't want your teammates, mostly all front-seat riders by now, to see you hoist yourself into a child safety seat in the back of Dad's van. Technically, you are old enough to ride up front, but physically you are still not big enough. Plus, Dad's van is all rickety and rusted and seems to move down the road all horked. You don't want anyone to see that, either, thinking less of you than they already do. Hockey is an expensive sport, and your parents aren't exactly rich. Not poor, but not rich. You know that Dad tries hard, does his best. And you love how he pulls those black leather gloves onto his hands. He clenches each fist methodically, patiently, then tugs down that boiled wool cap and adjusts it, just above those impenetrable black eyes. Like a hitman. That's how you like to think of your dad: Feared and revered. A total badass.

But you actually pity him now, forced to endure a son like you not wanting to be seen getting picked up in a car like his. You realize that this would make him sad: You so worried about looking poor, knowing how you feel about how you look wearing the constant hand-me-downs. About how the other boys, always with all their new stuff, their nicer things, think you're white trash.

More minutes pass and you've become bored watching your breath rings crystalize and suspend before you, each drifting away and dissipating magically. Like a wraith. Another new word you found by accident. You're still not sure you're saying it right, especially in the plural.

You need to keep moving to stay warm. The heat from the bungled scrimmage and warming house, now padlocked shut, has long left you. Your sweat-heavy clothing freezes stiff with hard crusted edges around your neck, arms, and chest. So you decide to walk out of the high school parking lot and start down the broken sidewalk on Ninth under the phone lines at Pine, still with a pair of sneakers draped over from Cernie's lucky toss last summer. Ahead lies the corner you know Dad will turn at. Head him off where Ninth crosses Cedar, that's your intent. Get into his crappy but very warm car faster. Any minute now.

It's darker out here. You've stepped from the reach of school lot lights into immediate blackness. The shift is like a fall from a sunny cliff. But it's been a mere step forward down Ninth Street, with just the one dim but familiar streetlamp a half block away on the other side.

A block away from the rink, you wonder about your teammates, and your *not-gay!*-brother, nearly sixteen. About how much time and energy he and his buddies dedicate to proving to one another and anyone else within earshot they're not gay. And about teammanship and if 'teammanship' is even a word. Something about the boys on your team that eludes you, something so ineffable about those boys and their brains. The way they think. And why they hate you so. Something irritating, confusing, distant, and itchy hangs in the air every time you are with the boys on the hockey team. Like you're some kind of exile. That's another word you recently discovered. Means to live away from one's native land, either by choice or by compulsion.

"Exile," you hear someone say. You look up and take one more step. A mass of snow and ice ruptures beneath your boot, a detonation scattering high-octave shards tinkling across the sidewalk ice. Normally you would snatch up one of these shards to peer at the moon through it, making the world disappear, even if only for a moment, through a sparkling kaleidoscope to another life. But not tonight because there is no moon. Just a river of bulging beads and trembling pearls about to drip from a sprawling black ocean above.

Instead, your eyes stop on a man leaning against a nearby telephone pole. You can smell him. Alcohol gasoline urine sweetness. Even in the dark of the new moon you can see he's soiled. Frozen grease splotches like oil- or blood spills on his jacket and dingy pants.

And you know. Or you think you know. Your dad has told you about people like this, mostly men.

But you wonder. Wonder how he got this way, homeless. You're not even sure what homelessness is or what it truly means. People are meant to live in homes, right? So what happened to his? Where did it go? How can he not have a place to live? And why doesn't he just get a hotel room or stay with a friend if his home is somewhere else far away like Milwaukee or Chicago?

The man wears only one boot, untied, his other foot wrapped in rags with a large wool (you think) sock pulled over, frayed pant cuff tucked in. One hand plunged into a jacket pocket, the other clutches a brown paper bag he now raises to his lips. This makes you think of Diekert, pacing around at the end of that rink, just getting through practice, swig by swig. You can't quite make out his face in the wedges of light offered by the lone streetlamp down the block, he's dark from the beard up. But you can tell he's looking right at you.

"Exile," you hear him say again. "Some things are just kinda hard to describe, aren't they?" he rasps. "But that's what I am. An exile."

This makes you forget the cold. You squint at him, this man with only one boot and precise speech. But there are no eyes there. Just blackness. You don't know what to say. You're a nice boy from Wisconsin, having been trained to respond to similar situations by simply allowing your good manners to take over. You swing your hockey bag from one shoulder to the other and address the man.

"Hello," you say, moving one step closer.

With a visible effort, the man shifts his weight. And you can tell he thinks you're rich. Of course he does. You have money for things like hockey sticks and rolls of tape, your hockey duffel now an absurd sack of luxury slung over your shoulder. But you're not rich. No one in your town, in fact, is rich. At least, you don't think so. Your hockey association can't even afford an indoor rink. You practice and play games out in the wind and cold and snow within a misshapen oval of broken boards the parents have the nerve to call a rink.

"How are you tonight," you ask.

"I'm leaning up against a post on a freezing-cold night," he says sharply. "How the f—" and he uses the f-word, in a colorful display of sarcastic inquiry to wonder just how it is, you believe, he is in fact, doing.

The f-word makes you recoil. It's different coming from him, not the same as when Eddie and his a-hole minions say it. They're still practicing compared to this guy. This man says the word like he owns it, with what actually could be hate, and you can smell it. Smell the hate coming from whatever it is inside that bag he keeps raising to a black void in the middle of his head just below his nose holes. It's his mouth, you realize, though it's unsettling the way his hairy skin collapses around the neck of the bottle. Like when you went to Florida with your parents and you saw an eagle ray consume a small squid near a tide pool. Peristalsis and osmosis via one mysterious orifice at the center of the ray's fluid fleshiness, a hairy vortex here right in front of you that pulls in hate from a bottle. Hate. That's what your dad calls it. Hate from a bottle.

You don't know how, but you are standing even closer to him now. Something draws you to him. Something against your will. It's not the cold. He holds a certain power over you because . . .

Exile. How does he know? How does he know what you were just now thinking? Is it that obvious? Mrs. Aspenes, your fourth-grade teacher, says you wear your heart on your sleeve, but you always thought that was just an expression. An *idiomatic* expression, in fact. That you blurt things out or maybe take everything too seriously. And it shows, Mrs. Aspenes says.

Exile. It's not him. It's you.

He's laughing. The man drinking hate from a bottle is laughing. Laughing a cold laugh that's one of world-weariness the guys only a few years older than you are trying so desperately to imitate or claim. You realize what you said was stupid and you decide to shut your big mouth for once and just keep quiet.

After a while, he still hasn't said another word. Neither have you.

The stillness of the clear night has crept into you now, and your father still hasn't come. The road he should be driving down remains wide, cold, dark, and empty. The last echoes of the last car to rumble past now long died away. Days ago, it seems.

The man raises the bottle to you. He gives it a twitch with a flick of his wrist. He's offering you a drink, you finally understand. You've had wine at Christmas a couple of times and it felt okay. It burned a little, but it wasn't so bad. Then you recall your cousin's wedding last summer. You threw up on the waiter after drinking two full glasses of champagne on your *not-gay!*-brother's dare. You want to back away from this man with one boot but can't. His arm is now fully extended, a brown paper clump in his hand twitching impatiently, urging you to accept.

You are a polite boy from Wisconsin. You should excuse yourself, now. And bid unto the man with one boot a pleasant evening. But your feet refuse to move.

An awareness engulfs you. This small act of walking down the street has unfolded into a huge decision that you will look back upon as a big moment in your life. Bigger than not passing the puck to Eddie Farrar, bigger than not kissing Monica Ritzing after school today when she wanted you to and no one would be looking. (Your only chance!)

Monica wouldn't do this. Neither would Eddie. And you know you shouldn't, either.

You pull the bottle away from your chapped lips and hand it back. Strangely, the contents of this bottle of hate don't taste like hate. So, for now, you disagree with your father. It's sorta sweet, actually. And kinda angry. Like toothpaste. Hate tastes like angry liquid toothpaste, you almost say aloud. You catch yourself as a smile is about to part your face, wondering what you were worried about, what Eddie would have been so scared of. Then that laugh of his, now like he's expecting you to leap into a fit of coughter. But you don't. Your eyes do go all blurry, though, and you bite your lip and he laughs again. Then, in response to the smile that started to split your face, your stomach revolts and catches fire. You hope you don't lose it again tonight, on the ride home in the back seat of Dad's van. Like that strawberry milkshake from McDonald's a couple of years ago on that one 106-degree day. Remember that? It got down behind your legs and into the folds of your car seat, and . . . Oh, God, Dad was pissed.

The man in the cold dark fades back into focus, and your mind drifts to Monica. It's hard not to have that happen. You think about her a lot. Eddie the a-hole, too. The man continues to look directly at you, and you find you cannot pull your eyes away from his.

"I wasn't always like this," he says.

His voice startles you. What he's said seems random enough that maybe the man feels the need to fill the silence. Like talking about the weather. Or the Packers. But the pitch of his voice has changed. Doesn't sound as raspy. Perhaps he feels he should share something more about himself in order to earn your trust.

"Where do you sleep?" you blurt. The question leaps from your lips so quickly it leaves you stunned, and you get the sense that things are starting to move in fast motion.

"Along the creek here in town. There's a woods below the old mill. Bunch of us live down there."

You nod. Of course. You thought all those guys were just camping down in those woods. But now that you think of it . . . they are always there, six or seven of them, every time you wander through with your fishing pole or whenever . . . at all times of the year. Always. You feel your jaw swing open. That's not their campsite . . . It's where they *live*.

You're old enough now to be completely embarrassed. That's one word you did not find by accident. Embarrassed: To feel awkwardly self-conscious and uneasy and unsettled. It's so cold that the man won't notice your blush, but he can see the arc in the change in your posture. He knows. You look back up at him.

"My wife got really sick a few years ago," he rasps. "She died."

And for the first time, it's him who looks away. The side of his head is completely black where there is no mouth or no eyes to occasionally reflect what little light there is to spare. You get the sense that maybe for just one moment he, too, is now aware of the spinning stars, the missing moon, and the deepening blackness above and all around. "Got fired because I was gone so much to be with her those last few months." He sniffs and wipes his face with the back of a hand. "Lucy." He looks away again and coughs and sniffs. "Then the bills came."

You don't know what to say. This shatters everything you have been taught about how the world works, which is basically all what your father has told you. Some of Mom, too. But almost all Dad. This homeless man had a wife. A wife with a name. Lucy. You turn your head to peer down the road for Dad. You try to imagine Dad like this. You can't. Not even close.

"Took my house, furniture, car, everything," the man says. Then he quickly clears his throat and looks up. He's looking at you again. "Moved here a few weeks ago. Getting a place this spring, though," he says. "Just started at Clem's. Should have enough saved up to rent a place by the time the weather breaks."

Clem's Garage. Of course. That explains the gasoline smell.

"Your ride's not here yet. So tell me . . . What happened?"

You're not certain what to say. But you recall how to answer adults when you want them to repeat something even though you indeed understood clearly what it is they said. It's a way to buy yourself time.

"Pardon me?" you say, but something about this man tells you that you know what he's about to get at.

He laughs quietly. He has yet to seem bothered by the cold. "Just now," he says. "Tonight. Seems like you're carrying around something more than just that duffel on your back." He raises his chin to indicate the bag slung over your shoulder.

You fill your lungs with the dark night and hold the cold down deep. You've heard about people's lungs crystallizing—freezing solid, even—in extremely cold weather, but you're pretty sure that that is just a story certain moms tell to keep their kids inside because seeing their kids outside on brutally cold days makes them feel cold, too, even as they sit inside and fret beside a crackling fire. The man tilts his head to a side, expectant.

"What happened out there," he asks.

You continue to hold your breath until you reach a silent count of forty-two. It's your favorite number. Actually, eleven is your favorite number. But you already passed it about twenty beats ago. Forty-two soon comes, though, and air rushes from your lungs and you stare down at your boots. Your head feels light from the angry liquid toothpaste and your stomach rumbles all hot and bothered and now your lungs ache. You look up from the sidewalk and tell the man about Eddie, the *wide-open* Eddie, about how you drew both defenders to you so expertly, and in the end, you did not pass the puck to him. Which was the entire point of all the work you did to lure the defenders to you in the first place.

"Why?"

You're out of breath, but you tell the man it's because Eddie is an a-hole. A giant a-hole, truth be told.

The man takes a drink. You try to laugh at your previous comment, but he interrupts you.

"And?" he says.

"That's it," you say. "He's an a-hole."

The man leans back against the telephone pole. "Huh," he says, and scratches at his face, those hairs that collapse around the neck of the bottle when he drinks.

"No such thing as a natural-born a-hole," he says. Except he doesn't say a-hole. He utters all the syllables of the entire word. You don't like where this is headed. Something inside you knows that telling him that Eddie is an a-hole and that's your story and you're sticking to it won't cut it. Not with this guy. And by now, in just the few minutes of talking to this man, your ears have stopped ringing every time you hear a word that you yourself shouldn't be saying. Something about the way this man is eyeing you now allows you to hear those forbidden syllables without mentally masking them. "Doctor doesn't hold a newborn up to the parents and say, 'Congratulations! You've given birth to a natural-born asshole.'"

This makes you laugh, and for good reason. Or reasons. One, it's funny, because two, he's right. Then you stop laughing because it jolts you that you've yet to really be able to talk to anyone about why it is you think Eddie is such an a-hole in the first place. Not your father. Not your mother. And definitely not your *not-gay!* brother. He is hostile and angry and far too wrapped up in proving to the planet that he is not gay.

Dad's van should come angling around the corner any second. But the street is still absorbing all available light and sound and remains eerily quiet and still.

"What's eating you about Eddie?"

You're still thinking about the man losing his home because his wife died. This is a sad thing to think about, and possibly the saddest thing you've ever heard, in fact.

But you're happy because it kept your mind off the heart of the why-Eddie-is-an-a-hole matter, even if only for a little while.

But now you clear your throat. The air is still and smooth and quiet as a stone. Like a stone you lift from the creek just upstream from where those men have actually been *living* all this time. You push back another rush of tears. You may as well tell him at this point.

Inside your jacket pocket is a fresh piece of gum, still in its wrapper. Will come in handy for when Dad picks you up. You hold it up for the man to see.

"I got this from Monica," you say.

You can't really see him, but you can tell he's smiling. "Ah, Monica."

"Well," and you realize that not only haven't you talked to anyone about this, but you've also yet to really even think about it. "She gave it to me for . . . after school."

"Ah. And how did that go?" The man takes a drink from his bottle. He doesn't seem as homeless now. There's a new intensity to the air and all those faster-flowing stars whirling around you. Everything seems to be moving at a quicker pace. Except you. You aren't cold and your feet have not moved. And you are talking to this now not-as-homeless man who once had a wife and now wants to know your story.

"It didn't," you say.

You get the sense that he knew you were going to say that. He clears his throat and cocks his head. "Why not?"

And now things are moving so fast you almost can't see. You find yourself talking all at once, and all in one cold breath. You're pretty certain there's a word you found one day to describe this phenomenon, but you can't think of it now because your ears are ringing but it's not from anyone swearing, it's from saying something you don't want to hear yourself say but you know that you can't help but say it. Being able to summon that word would relax you enough to be able to continue better. But you can't. So you have to stumble on with your mouth.

"When she gave me the gum, she said to make sure to chew it right before we met up so that I didn't have stinky breath like Eddie did when she kissed him the day before behind the clump of oaks."

You exhale and look down at your boots. A clump of trees is called a copse. You wish there was a chunk of ice to shatter like the one that exploded beneath your boot right before you saw this man. But things are different now. There's just you there, stuck with yourself, and this kind man with one boot and his dead wife who had a name and seems to be hovering all around you. Lucy.

"I see," he says. He clears his throat. "That explains why you didn't pass the puck. Not that he's an asshole but that Monica kissed him first." He sniffs. "You're jealous."

Your silence tells him he's right. Your eyes fill and sting with angry tears. You hate when that happens. None of the guys seem to get it that the fury someone feels due to the outright stupidity of any one thing can make you cry. You're able to hold it back, but you know that the man can see the stars glinting off the tears welling in your eyes.

"Went through the same thing," the man says. "With Lucy."

You shake your head like you don't understand.

"Of course I did," he says, and smiles again. "Took me forever to make peace with the idea that she'd had the hots for other guys before she met me."

Your stomach turns, and not because of the sweet angry liquid toothpaste roiling in your guts. The idea of your mom ... *dating* ... anyone other than your dad...

"Now, let me guess. This Monica ... is really pretty."

You nod.

"And the guys buzz around her like bees."

You nod again.

"Normal that if you find a girl pretty others will, too, don't you think?" He coughs. You don't say anything. He points a finger at you. "Important thing is that she still wants to kiss *you*." He lowers his arm and shakes his head. "Took me a while to figure that one out." He shakes his head again. "God, I was a stupid asshole."

You stare at him. You can't put it in to words, exactly, but calling himself a stupid a-hole just now is partly his way of telling you that you are behaving the same way. And a sleepy wave of relief flows over you. Monica still wants to kiss you ... *after* she'd already kissed Eddie Farrar! Suddenly your lungs don't hurt as much, your shoulders loosen, and your eyes stop stinging. You focus on the powdery white clouds of the Milky Way over the man's shoulder. The dark sky so black and so close. Things are going to be okay. You're gonna figure this out. A smile of relief teases up your cheek.

"Going to be very hard for you now, though," he says, and shakes his head sadly. Your breath catches, and your eyes start to sting again.

"How?" you yelp.

"You shoulda passed the puck."

You groan.

"You pissed off Eddie, lost the match, and now once Monica hears about it—and you can bet she will—you won't get a chance to kiss her for a very long time." He sniffs and wipes his nose and tilts his chin up the way Dad does when he is about to finish making an important point. "If ever."

A weighty emptiness flattens you. You hate when someone else's clarity does this. A simple turn of phrase that renders you utterly speechless, more speechless than the pathetic wall-crawler that you already are. You with your sliced-dread-on-white-bread sandwiches. Some nights the blackness of the sky is closer than others. Tonight you want it to stay low and dark and heavy forever.

"Your ride," the man says, the blackness above his neck, his head, motioning to a void behind your shoulder, "has arrived." He tucks the bottle under his arm and places the hand that was holding the bottle into his jacket pocket. He turns his shoulders and nods to you as you sense him slip away. "Good luck, my friend," he says.

And it occurs to you that somehow this man can move the dark. Like pushing a coin across a table with only your thoughts, he can grasp darkness between his fingertips. Or perhaps he's clutching on to it with the hand that remained inside his coat pocket this entire time. Either way, you're convinced he got here by opening a crack in the blackness and stepping out to join you in your mutual exile. Greet you and share a drink and set you straight. And that soon he'll disappear back inside. You know it.

The coughter finally comes, and you realize you are looking at the ground, eyes filling, when you notice your dad's van round the corner and bank down the street toward you. You, with nothing to hide, really, apart from one selfish, a-holeian play at the end of scrimmage. Nothing to hide at all.

Except your breath. Quickly you unwrap Monica's stick of gum and shove it into your mouth and start chewing fast. Some hot cinnamon-flavor that really burns.

Your father's van eases to a stop next to you. Dad doesn't roll down the window, just beckons from inside with a few pumps of a gloved hand. It's dark and all you can see is the deeper darkness of the man with one boot reflected off the windows of your dad's van, but you know that's what your dad's doing inside. Beckoning. With a slightly pained expression. It's the face he can always be counted on to make. A face you're glad no one can see.

The spicy gum makes your eyes water. But they've already been watering tonight, and not just from the cold.

Now you nod to Dad, thinking quickly that you should breathe, like your *not-gay!* brother once advised you, through your nose only. Like after you sneak sips of brandy from Dad's liquor cabinet. Behind you, the man slips from his post. You don't hear him leave. He parts a seam in the dark and steps through the barrier into a beyond some*where* and possibly some *time* else, you think. Peristalsmosis, perhaps. All you hear is the popping crunch of sub-zero snow beneath the tires of your father's van, then complete silence and the return of stillness. You sense Dad beckoning again.

Dad stopped apologizing for being late over a month ago. Now, he just asks how practice went. And normally, you give him all the highlights. But tonight you are still staring into the darkness, tracing with your eyes a path the man with only one boot may have taken. But this new moon is very dark. Dark where he walked, dark where he shared his story, dark inside the belly of wherever it is he just went, dark where you finally found someone to talk to, and dark in the bedroom where Monica Ritzing, fragrant and warm beneath her cozy quilts, will soon ease to sleep.

You tell Dad that practice was okay and ask him about his day. He looks at you in the rear-view mirror, and rather than answer, he asks who you were just now talking to. He must have seen the two of you in the bounce of headlights.

"Some guy," you say. And it occurs to you that you don't even know the man's name. His dead wife Lucy, yes. But not the man. "I am Arthur," you murmur at the window. "I am," you whisper to the post he disappeared from. You're not sure why you're saying that, but it feels good. So you thump your chest and murmur it again. "I am."

"You were talking to a stranger?"

"He works at Clem's."

"Arthur!" Dad scolds. "You know better." He looks out the driver-side window, straining to see the man who slipped away into a crease in the dark. "People like that," Dad starts, and jams the van into Park. He turns around to speak to you. "People like that," he says, and you almost immediately stop hearing. You don't need to know about people like that anymore because you've met one. Up close and personal and on the street. You know his story. Your eyes blur. Partly because Monica's crazy-hot cinnamon gum is making your eyes water, partly because you have no more brain space for this with your dad right now. Not now. So you just nod and nod and nod until he stops. That's generally a good strategy.

"Okay?" he's been saying. "Oh-*kay*?"

You stare at him blankly.

He raises his voice slightly. Dad's not a yeller. Not his style in the least. So when he does yell, it grabs your attention. "Have you been listening, Arthur?"

You nod again and say, "Okay, Dad."

"Well, alright," he says, and turns to face forward. You can tell he's not satisfied, and you know that in the end, he's just looking out for you and your own good. It's all he knows. Constant worry. Constant. He sighs and rests his forehead on the back of a gloved hand that clutches the steering wheel, and you wonder if it's worth it, really, to have kids.

He drops the van into Drive.

You snap your gum and tighten your abs to prepare to pull away. But it's no use. Your stomach plummets as Dad's van jerks forward into the dark darkness. And from here it's clear that your darkness may as well be eternal, that it will remain dark everywhere you happen to step, everywhere you happen to look, and everywhere you happen to think.

Randy Koenig's Very Large Mouse

I wasn't surprised that Randy acted as though he didn't really care that he had mice in his house. He was the sort of guy for whom mice were simply a part of home ownership.

Another likely reason he didn't care was that this was the first gathering for any of us since the start of the COVID-19 pandemic, and the possibility of some mice running around the place didn't seem to matter so much. After all, we all had mice, and a mouse here and there couldn't top the overall rush of relief we felt about being able to move beyond the pandemic and participate in organized society again. For a "return to normal," as everyone kept saying, and moreover, not to have died.

I walked into his home through the back door, the first house other than mine that I had entered in sixteen months, bearing an ice-cold twelve-pack of Night Rain beer. Randy pointed at a closed door and told me to put it in the fridge down in the root cellar. I nodded and he raised his voice above the crowd to get my attention. That's when he mentioned the mice.

"Oh, yeah," another guest said. "I just saw one when I was down there." Michelle wore a tight t-shirt and baggy sweatpants with holes worn through the knees. "Easily the biggest mouse I've ever seen," she said. She placed her hands on her hips and looked over at Randy. They laughed.

"Yeah," Randy said. "I saw a pretty big one down there the other day, too." He squatted before a kitchen cupboard and reached inside, banging pots.

"Put out any traps?" someone else said.

"Not yet," Randy said. He stood upright. "It's only been a couple of days. And I really haven't had time." He set a metal colander in the sink. "Besides," he said, and raised his eyebrows, "I think that big one's gonna need a special kinda trap."

"What?" another said. There were so many people here. I didn't know the woman who just spoke by name. She moved in across the street just before the pandemic got dire, and we'd only exchanged friendly waves from opposite sides of our street ever since. She looked at me with a confused smile.

"Yeah," Randy said. He started to dig around in another cupboard. "Gonna hafta call someone, I think," he said. "It's a biggin."

I started down the steps.

"Fridge is near the back," Michelle called down after me. "Light switch is this one dangling string near the bottom," she said. "Just wave your hand around. You'll find it." She closed the door behind me, deadening all the upstairs chatter and laughter.

My pulse quickened in the complete and immediate chill of the underground darkness, and I felt my pupils dilate as I gripped the railing and descended into the black root-cellar aromas and humidity. Something like gossamer brushed my cheek. I gasped. Too many scrambling legs made their way up toward my ear and shot around the back of my head.

Turns out the lithe thing dragging across my face was the light switch cord. My fingertips traced the too-many-legged thing to a large knot at the end, and pulled. A weak forty-watt glow sprawled across the room at a speed that seemed far less than I normally expected the speed of light to travel. I had to think about that possibility for a moment. And how the extreme isolation of the pandemic had distorted so many of my senses and perceptions.

The beer fridge was pressed between a sink and a washing machine along the far wall, and I had to weave between laundry baskets and an ironing board to get to it. And I wondered: Does the light emitted by certain sources travel more slowly than others? How does that affect one's perceived version of reality?

I swung the door of the fridge open and was stopped by a rustling sound behind me. I turned and stared.

Now, most people aren't truly scared of mice. Mice, taken alone, and in a controlled environment, are actually pretty cute. But a wall that jumps unexpectedly in your peripheral vision—in a dimly lit root cellar—can startle you. Then those shiny, beady eyes that catch the light a certain way . . . But nothing on the gigantic mouse that sat down at a table behind me was small enough to call *beady*. It was so large.

I gasped audibly. The word *rat* escaped my lips.

The creature raised up to look at me. It scratched at its chin, and I noticed its eyes narrow.

"Everyone says that," the thing said, and started to chuckle. "But no. I am a mere mouse." He paused to stretch and scratch an ear. "Granted," the mouse said, "the biggest fucking mouse you've ever seen, right here in Randy Koenig's basement." He spoke with a deep voice and with precise diction. Upper-Midwestern accent. "But still just a mouse nonetheless."

I blinked.

"Should get those in the fridge," the mouse said, and nodded at the twelve-pack that remained tucked under my arm.

I blinked again.

"But pull one out first," he said. "You're probably ready for one, am I right?"

I continued to stare and blinked and nodded.

"Relax," he said. "You're not crazy." The mouse sat upright and rested an elbow on the table and scratched at his chin again. "A rat," he scoffed. "Please. Not even close."

I had to admit that I'd never thought about how a mouse may differ from a rat, apart from size.

He leaned back in his chair and reached for a box of crackers on a shelf over his shoulder. Randy's Pandemic Pantry. Everyone had one: A three-week supply of foodstuffs from which one could conjure a meal in the event of another state-enforced lock-down. Like most of my friends, Randy Koenig probably only left the house once every ten days to re-stock. Shelter-in-place, we called it. But now, with COVID-19 in apparent retreat across America, it was clear Randy had been eating down his pantry.

I was still staring when the mouse said, "So . . . Are you going to say something?" He tore the box of crackers open with his teeth and then carefully removed a sleeve of saltines. He grasped an edge and pulled it open along the seam with the tips of his paws. He looked back up at me. "Well? A greeting? Or a salutation, perhaps?"

"Jesus Christ," I gasped.

"No," the mouse said, "that's not what I go by. My name actually—"

"No," I said. "I mean, *how* did you open that wrapper like that?"

The mouse held up its paws and wiggled its digits. Like a pianist showing off his goods. "Dunno," the mouse said, and shrugged. "Like this?" He gave me a confused look and carefully plucked a cracker from the stack and raised it before him. "How would *you* do it?"

"But you're a *mouse*," I said. "Which means—"

"Oh, very good! Glad you got the mouse part down," he laughed.

I laughed, too, and felt myself relax.

"No. I mean, that as a mouse, you shouldn't be able to grab onto something like that."

"I shouldn't?" he said. This seemed to surprise the mouse. "No kidding." He arranged more crackers on the table and looked up at me. "Imagine that," he said. He gestured and offered me a cracker.

I hesitated.

"It's fine," he said. "I washed my paws before sitting down. See?" he said, and held up his opened paws for my inspection.

I nodded. "Thanks," I said, and took one. It was fresh and crunchy.

"Here," the mouse said. "Have another." The mouse paused to nudge the stack toward me. "Please. I don't mind."

I washed down the next cracker with a swallow of beer. "What I was going to say is that you don't have opposable thumbs. How on earth could you grasp the wrapper like that in order to pull it apart?"

The mouse shrugged and started to build another stack of crackers beside the one we had been eating from.

"Beats me," he said. "But look. You're here down in Randy's root cellar drinking beer and having a conversation with possibly the largest mouse ever to have lived on this planet . . . and you're wondering about opposable thumbs?"

29

"It's just so unbelievable," I said.

"But you're cool with the whole chatting-with-a-boy-sized-mouse thing," he said.

The mouse had a point. And he was correct: he was approximately the size of an eight-year-old boy. I mean, this thing was *huge*. His whiskers were the size of drinking straws, and drooped from his snout like strings of black spaghetti. He had a *neck*. And . . . *shoulders*. And somehow the ability to sit upright in a chair and cross his legs.

I walked over to the light switch string that brushed my face on the way down, and pulled. The room went dark again. I waited a few seconds before turning the light back on. The light seemed to reach the far wall more quickly this time.

The mouse lifted another cracker and waved at me from where he stacked the saltines. "Hi," he called out. "Still here," he said. "Ain't goin nowhere." The mouse smiled.

"Jesus Christ," I said again.

The mouse laughed and nibbled. He gestured for me to take another cracker. I did.

"Where do you live," I asked, turning my head side to side to locate a place large enough for him to fit into. "There's nowhere…"

"In the limestone," the mouse said. He gestured behind him. "Underground. Between basements."

I tilted my head inquisitively. "In the limestone," I said.

"Yep," the mouse said. "My family and I shuttle between basements all up and down this ridge. It's all limestone," he said. "And the basements are all basically just etched from one long stratum of sedimentary rock."

"Jesus Christ," I said again.

"What? You didn't know this?" the mouse said, and threw up his paws in disgust. "Why do the humans around here act so surprised to learn that their basements are all connected? 'Randy Koenig's got centipedes,' one of the neighbors will snigger, because she doesn't want people to know that she's got centipedes, too. And here's the deal," the mouse said. He looked me squarely in the eyes, and I could tell he was about to make an important point. "It's the same centipedes! They just scuttle up and down the street, from house to house to house and back. Infinite little cracks, passageways, channels, and caverns span miles upon miles along this ridge, occasionally interrupted by the basement of a human dwelling." He waved a paw before him. "Like this one."

I nodded and listened to him nibble the corner of a cracker while he watched me take all this in. After a while, I said, "How do you get through the walls? I mean you're so ... *big*."

"Yeah. Well, it turns out that despite all of my enormity, I am, in the end, still a mouse."

I shrugged.

"You really don't know much about mice, do you?" the mouse said. "Apart from your belief that I shouldn't be able to lift a cracker like this," he said, and carefully grasped another saltine between two digits of his left paw.

I shrugged.

"So, in being a mouse, I can wriggle through nearly any opening, no matter how small it may be," he said. "As long as my nose fits."

I shook my head again, then wondered about the neighbors he mentioned. "So, do you spend much time in the other homes?"

"Some days. Randy's got a nice place here. Very organized." The mouse paused to wipe a few crumbs from his snout. "So it's not hard to linger while the Missus is off doing other stuff," he said, and quickly turned his gaze down to the back of his wrist to check his watch. "But I had heard there was a party here tonight. So."

I didn't bother to ask how he managed to tell time.

"The Jonstruds have more stuff," the mouse said. I saw the mouse's eyeballs flick from shelf to shelf, wall to wall. "A lot more, actually. But Randy's got it all more organized. I mean, I feel like I wouldn't forget what I came in here for when I walk into Randy Koenig's basement pantry."

I glanced around again. "True," I said. "Seems as though he's been eating it down, however." I tried to recall the current state of my pantry—garbanzo beans, olive oils, oats—but nothing clear really came to mind.

"Indeed," the mouse said. "That has not gone unnoticed. The pandemic was good for the Missus and me in that way— all the basements along this ridge were so well stocked." He looked around again. I think he sighed. "Plus, we've had to change our routine. People have been active at all hours of the night, and they don't go anywhere during the day anymore." I watched him pause to chew more crackers. "The result is constant human activity in every one of these homes." He made a gesture to what I assumed was the outside street. "So we had to adapt to become less nocturnal." He stretched and yawned. "And now . . . it seems like we're just so tired all the time."

I considered this for a minute. Was it inconsiderate of me to assume that the pandemic only had an effect on people? My dog came to mind. Poor thing nearly loses her mind every time I leave her alone for more than an hour. She's going to need some kind of therapy once I return to full-time commuting, too. I looked back at the mouse and nodded.

"But not so much anymore. I mean," the mouse said, "don't get me wrong. There's still plenty to eat." He chuckled and gestured to the bare shelves behind him again. "But at this rate of pantry depletion, me and the Missus may have to adapt a more nomadic lifestyle."

The mouse yawned and stretched. "And with so much food always around, it seems that all I've wanted to do during this pandemic is eat," he said. He patted his round belly with a palm. "Constantly."

There was a thump and a muffled whoop from upstairs. We both looked up.

"Ever run up there?" I said.

"Never," the mouse said, solemnly. He closed his eyes and folded his arms and shook his head. "Not once."

Back upstairs, everything seemed normal again. The party was busy. More guests had arrived, music played loudly, and people laughed and hugged. They spoke of their jobs, their hair, their weight-gain, an end to virtual schooling for their kids. I glanced at the root-cellar door behind me. Had I imagined the entire enormous-mouse thing? I must have, I decided. The pandemic had been so hard and so weird for all of us. One prolonged distortion of time and reality, and not in a good way.

Michelle asked where I'd been all this time.

"The root cellar," I said, and before I could stop myself, I mentioned that I'd seen a rather large mouse while down there.

"Ah," Randy said, overhearing. He turned his head from an upper cupboard. "Musta seen the one I saw." He laughed quietly. "Pretty big, eh?" he said, in that musing and indifferent way of his.

"Yeah," I said, and took a bite of a saltine cracker that the mouse had given me. I listened briefly to the music, the laughter, and the chatter before responding. Things were indeed feeling more normal again. "Biggest mouse I've ever seen."

Larmet Lunker

On the banks of the Larmet River, my brother Michael told me all kinds of stories about the War. The people, the land, the food. I told him I had never caught a trout over nine inches long. He said that Vietnam was beautiful and that nine inches sounded about right considering I was just nine years old. Most beautiful place he'd ever seen, he said. Perfect for getting blown to bits.

He showed me Polaroids of him and his buddies. I scanned the far riverbank for a good spot to cast my line. They were always seated in a tavern, always with beers in hand, always Vietnamese girls perched on laps. Sometimes my bait got hung up in the trees. Always the same girl for Michael. We either had to wade over to untangle my line, or cut it off. Michael didn't want to get into the water too often after he got back, and I was too small to wade into a lot of the spots I was casting at. I was going after a lunker, which meant deep water. I looked at more of his pictures. We usually cut the line. The girl disappeared toward the end of the stack. His smile in the photos got different after that.

I asked what her name was. Michael's eyebrows twitched up. A moment later, he lowered his gaze and looked away and said her name into some tall grass. There was a breeze and rapids and weeds swishing, so I didn't hear. I looked at the tall grass, too. The blades were bright green and beaded with ladybugs and dew.

She was pretty. I never asked if he wrote to her. But I wondered.

The war gore was constant, my eyes always huge as he told me about guys with arms or legs or parts of their face blown off. Michael walking around carrying someone else's arm or eyeball back. Jesus Christ, he'd say, throwing his head back. The eyes, he said. Ya had to bring the eyes back. Eyes are what make a guy, ya know? Jesus Christ almighty.

One day he told me about the bullets streaming down from the sky while I put a nightcrawler onto a size eight hook. Seriously like rain, he said. The nightcrawler squirmed between my fingers, impaled. Bullets missed whatever they were shot at way up on this one hill, and fell down and whacked the Quonset hut he and his Company all slept and ate in. Like hail, he said. Michael told me to be sure to leave some of the nightcrawler's tail wiggling free. You knot them up so much, he said.

The bullets bounced off the Quonset mostly harmlessly, he said. But you still didn't want to walk outside into that. He told me not to walk so heavy on the riverbanks. I thought I was being stealthy.

That's why you only catch the little ones, he explained. You scare off all the keepers. Foot-falls create sounds heard only by fish. Sound travels way faster under water, he said. He stretched his arms out wide and wiggled his fingers like ripples.

Later he pointed to a nice undercut bank and held his breath, no doubt hoping that my cast wouldn't get hung up in the prickly ash bushes that bent into the river. "Prickly ash" is a really good name for those things.

Next time on the river he told me about a huge boat they had him stationed on for a really long time. The size of a city block. There was not a whole lot for them to do while at sea. They were waiting for orders, he said. But one day they got to blow up an enemy ship. They split it in half with a deafening shell from over a mile away and watched it fold into the sea through a telescope. Otherwise, he said he got really fat on that boat. So fat he hoped he wouldn't get sent home because our dad had a thing about fat people.

One morning it was really hot on the Larmet. Michael picked me up at 4:30. I remember him shaking me awake, his sour breath on my face, his gold chain swinging from his neck. I was sweating before the sun came all the way up. He parked and we split up for a while. The nettles were just tall enough and just prickly enough to make pushing a path along the riverbank very unfun. I was just about to ease into a new fishing spot I'd found when I heard a distant whoop. Michael. Several whoops. A lunker.

I made my way to him as fast as I could, but couldn't find him anywhere on the river. I finally went back to his car. Took forever. I pulled off my waders and looked around. His fancy wide-collared button-down shirt lay draped over the hood of his car. And there was Michael, sprawled out bare-chested and asleep in the back seat, a thick forearm shielding his eyes. His hands were black with river dirt, the knees of his white bell-bottom jeans soiled and stained a dark green.

Michael? I said.

He groaned and rolled onto a side. I said his name again but he didn't move. I pulled a can of Coke from his cooler. It was still morning, Mom would be mad, but I didn't care. I was boiling hot and itchy all over from fighting nettles.

I was also really confused: Here we were trout fishing on the famous Larmet River, my brother had just caught a lunker, and he was sleeping through it. How could anyone possibly sleep through that?

Michael nearly jumped out of his skin when I snapped the can open. He bolted upright and yelled and screamed something I couldn't understand. He knocked me over as he ran to the river and shoved his head in the water. I picked up my Coke.

He walked back from the riverbank slowly, and pulled his wet hair back over his head. He was growing it out. He told me about arms and eyeballs again, and repeated the story about spent bullets hitting the Quonset huts. All the people on that ship they sank.

I asked about the whooping.

Oh, he said. That was me?

I nodded.

No kidding, he said. He rubbed the stubble on his chin and scratched at his lamb-chop sideburns. Huh, he murmured.

He had this far-off look in his eyes. I knew not to say anything.

Well, he said. I buried her.

I shook my head. You what?! I yelled. You *buried*—

Tuyen deserved a decent burial, he said. He stared at the long, wet weeds again and shrugged. She did, he insisted. He reached absently for my can of Coke. C'mon, he said. Let's go to Mary's.

I wanted to see that fish in the worst way. Something live and fleshy from the glossy pages of *Field & Stream*. But we sped away, kicking up gravel.

Michael ate two Specials. I figured he didn't get food like Mary's Café while at the War. I ordered pancakes and eggs but I couldn't eat the eggs because the cook made them sunny-side up. Michael laughed and ate my eggs for me. I told him about wanting to catch a lunker and have it mounted on my bedroom wall before he got back from Vietnam. Like a surprise. He scraped his plate and got coffee.

After a while, he said we could dig it up and tell everyone I caught it. I didn't like the idea, but I said okay anyway.

We parked in our usual spot by the Larmet. He parted the soil with his hands and lifted her carefully from layers of dirt and lush grasses.

What Michael pulled from the black earth along the Larmet River that blistering-hot morning was pure magic. A gleaming twenty-four inch brownie that could only belong to another world.

I gasped. So beautiful, I said.

Yes, he murmured. I thought I heard his breath catch. She was, he whispered.

He took me home going ninety. Kept saying to put the trout in the freezer right away, that you gotta freeze it properly before getting it stuffed.

Michael dropped me off. Said he was headed to a barbecue. No need to stop by his place because, Heck, he said, I'm already dressed!

He laughed and laughed and peeled away, shooting gravel.

I still had the trout clutched to my chest while the gravel shot up. I put Michael's lunker in the basement freezer and rode my bike to the ball fields and played with my friends until supper.

That night, Michael buried her again in my sleep.

My teenage sisters' crying woke me really early the next morning. I stumbled out of my room straight into a wall. Hay fever sealed my eyelids shut during the night. I had to press water into the gunk over the bathroom sink to get them open. I wobbled toward the kitchen, eyes all gauzy, and saw two police officers sitting on living room chairs. Dad leaned against the big hi-fi by the picture window, motionless, and stared out at the dawn piercing the trees. My tall sisters with long messy hair and flowing nightgowns leaned into each other on the couch. They choked and gasped and moaned. I thought I'd awoke in someone else's house or was still asleep and had wandered from my dream into a different person's. I filled a glass with water while my mom sat on the floor against the wall of the living room, knees pulled to her chest, rocking beneath the slurred murmurs of cops.

The room got really quiet when I walked in from the kitchen. The doorbell rang. Everyone turned their head.

I was the only one up, so I answered the door. A priest on the other side peered through the screen. Felt like Confession, him on the other side of that mesh, so serious, forehead wrinkled into rows of eyebrows. Rosary beads swung from a Bible pressed to his chest, and clacked. I didn't recognize him. He was older. But he wore the same clothes, and had the same waxy skin, and same stale breath of our regular priest.

After a pat on my head and a cup of my chin, he crossed over to my mom. She lowered her fists from her eyes and shrieked and crumpled onto her side.

I ran away downstairs and crashed into the chest freezer. I had to leave. The horrible wailing, the strange men in our house. But I also knew I had to make sure Michael's trout was okay. Tuyen. Maybe get back into my dream—if I'd even left it—to be sure.

I raised the lid on the freezer and gazed at that frozen magical fish. Its golden frosted sides, the bright white belly.

And the crimson and black spots that lit up beneath my touch. Gorgeous brown trout. I couldn't believe I'd forgotten about her while at the ball fields the day before, the way Michael said her name while unearthing her from beneath those weeds: Tuyen.

I pulled her from the freezer and sat down and placed her between my legs. Like I would a pail of ice cream. I stared. But not for long. I didn't want to have to re-freeze her before Michael came by to head over to the taxidermist.

I pressed my thumbs onto her dark eyes, melting the layer of frost until they glowed fleshy beneath my skin. I curled up on my side next to her. Tuyen's eyes shone before me, looking up at Michael as he lifted her from the soil, opened her nest of fresh blades of grass. I saw her rise and sit on Michael's lap, Michael murmuring her name, and Tuyen saying it wasn't his fault, not his fault, her deep wet eyes easing mine closed on the basement floor beside Michael's Larmet lunker.

little blind flying mice

A timeline for bat removal—that's what they demanded when they knocked on my door. Two City Hall officials stood in my doorway, perspiring in the late-summer heat, and explained that they'd come to inquire about my plan for "the abnormal abundance of bats" living in my attic.

"My plan," I asked, taken aback.

I'd planned to leave the bats alone. They would eventually hibernate or migrate. And in the meantime, they seemed perfectly content to go on devouring more than their body weight in insects per night. An army of mosquito-eaters— what was wrong with that?

"Meeting's in two days," said the older one. Thin hair, peeling red scalp. "Eight o'clock at the Community Center." He leaned to a side and looked over my shoulder into my kitchen, then back up at me. "It would be in your best interests to be there."

I watched them walk away, ugly memories fluttering about my brains.

The bats entered my life last spring, a few weeks after Jerome died.

"Cardiac arrest," my neighborhood vet, Mandy, said as she covered the body of my beloved basset hound, Jerome. I told her about how the Jack Russell came out of nowhere, a black-and-white snarling bowling ball that charged around the corner of a hedgerow and tore into the back of Jerome's neck. Jerome howled, I screamed, and when I reached down for the Jack Russell's collar, it seized my hand in its surprisingly powerful jaws. The pain was deep, immediate, and intense. Though I did manage to punt the thing off me rather quickly.

End over end that Jack Russell arced into the street, where he bounced once and yelped twice before getting flattened by a speeding pickup truck that screeched to a too-late stop. Dead on impact from the truck's front axle, doubly-dead death assured by the subsequent crunch of ribs beneath a rear tire. My dear Jerome, meanwhile, had collapsed onto his side behind me and died with a whimper. The driver of the pickup staggered out and shook all over and touched his face again and again, slurring and groaning. He swung his head back and forth, around and around, and finally flopped over, sprawled like a sack of busted flour into the bed of his still-idling F-150.

"Ned?" Mandy said, hesitantly. I heard her, but my mind was still miles away from her office. "*Ned,*" she repeated, startling my senses.

"Ooooh," she cooed, and lowered her eyelids. "What a *terrible* experience." I nodded. Perhaps I was in shock. My dearest and only dog I ever owned dead, my throbbing hand very badly maimed, and the stroked-out driver of the truck later pronounced dead on arrival at the University's Medical Center ER. Not to mention the flattened Jack Russell.

I nodded again and shuffled down the trail of stone pavers leading from her clinic, my sweet dog's dead snout resting in the crook of my arm.

Two weeks later, the first of my bats introduced itself.

Tonight at the Town Hall meeting my sweating City Hall visitors told me about, a half dozen of my bats loop in wobbling coils high above my head beneath the vaulted ceilings of the Noisy Creek Community Center. They know that soon I'll flip the switch that turns on the multi-colored LED bulbs woven into my spiked hair. Their signal it's time to leave. Until then, they will idle about in silent flight, drifting from one alcove to another of this former house of worship. The rest of my bats are outside, feeding away in chattering swirls.

"I never asked for these bats," I say to the packed and skittish gathering. "They just started ... following me around one night." I stop there, because it seems clear there's no space to explain what's really been going on.

All eyes are upon me, but I'm still glancing around, noticing that this place hasn't changed a bit in at least twenty-five years: The worn and ragged rugs tossed onto the beaten floorboards, the sagging walls, the bitter aroma of burnt coffee, the brownish water-damage stains blooming across the ceiling tiles in a series of Rorschach tests (answer: "Bats," obviously), and the yellowed wall sconces still emitting a feeble source of buzzing light. Two oval window frames on the far wall carve deep eyes into the dark of night.

A man in the front row rises from his seat into the middle of an episode of *Little House on the Prairie*. He turns to address us, his fellow *Little House* parishioners. "We residents of Noisy Creek," he declares, in a rehearsed manner, "need to take a stand"—*stee-yand*, he says, like the good upper-Midwesterner he is—"against this inundation of bee-yats!"

Heads nod mechanically as a murmur ripples through the crowd. My bats pause like a slowing engine and hover, suspended mid-flap in a way that only bats can.

"These little . . . wing-ed . . . *demons*," he says, glancing above him. My bats resume their swirls.

"I'm just terrified I'll get one caught in my hair!" a woman calls out. She raises a hand to her face. People seated nearby nod and sigh.

"They're just . . . gross!" A hiss from near the front. Brent, I think. There's enough people and enough noise up there now that it's getting hard to tell who's saying what. "They're . . . they're…"

"Evil!" a woman cuts in to finish.

"It's a sign!" the man next to her groans, and raises opened palms to the vaulted ceilings. "A sign!"

And I'm pretty sure it's Brent who blurts, "Filthy . . . rats!"

A silence broken only by the fluid pulsing of my idling bats' wings seizes the room.

Now, one could regard a comparison of bats to rats as unseemly, but actually, according to my bats, Brent wouldn't be the first ever to draw a line connecting the two. And, once pulled apart by its Latin roots, the Spanish word for bat, *murciélago*, literally unpacks itself to mean "little blind flying mouse." But the Spanish, my bats tell me, were just having some fun with the bats' curious bug-snatching flight patterns when they came up with that. There's nothing wrong with bats' eyes. They see perfectly well. Nearly as well as humans. They just choose to hunt at night, when they rely more heavily on echolocation than sight.

"We need to take a stee-yand!" Little Homer on the Prairie states again. He leaps to his feet and looks around (possibly for Nellie Olson). He swallows and runs a few fingers through what's left of his comb-over and pumps a fist with each word: "Against. These. Bee-yats!"

46

"Bats have no interest in your hair, honey," Harriet calls out in a smoldering voice. She adjusts the teetering silo of a grayed copper mane stacked atop her head to underscore her point. Harriet, a nationally renowned Professor Emerita of Chemistry here at the University of Wisconsin-Noisy Creek, lives around the corner from me on Vinny Street. She's a powerful presence and I fear, for now, what she's about to say. My bats tell me there's no need to fear, though, but who knows. Harriet is capable of just about—

"And I recommend," Harriet sighs, "you all do some reading on the matter of bats prior to deciding on anything remotely drastic. Educate yourselves," she says, returning to her seat, "about bats."

What a relief! So glad an authority in science can verify what my gut (and my bats) tell me to be so true: *My bats are harmless.*

I'm starting to think that's that with this meeting when a guy named James decides he's got something to say after all.

"Problem I got with all this, Ned," he says, with an apologetic tone. It's a slow voice that's laden with tough-love and regret. "Problem I got is kids round town thinkin it's sorta 'cool,'" he says, curling his fingers held high to surround *cool* with exaggerated air quotes. My bats pause, fanning mid-air like fish in a tank. "You walkin round . . . them LED lights in your hair . . . with all them bats."

"They *do!*" a man nearby hollers, jumping up. "They think it's cool! My kids dragged the Christmas lights outta the basement storage and got all wrapped up in them coupla nights ago!" He holds his arms out and takes a few steps, knees locked, in a manner, I'm supposing, of a marching Christmas tree. "I . . . I mean . . . It's just . . . What the hell?"

He turns towards us, exasperated, arms still held straight out as though nailed to a cross.

"Sets a bad example," James says, and shakes his head. He shares a nod of kinship with the man. James clasps his hands behind his hips and looks down, rocking slowly on the sides of his feet.

I start to respond to that comment when a woman's voice I recognize cuts me off. Nora.

"*My* kids," she says, "wanted to do the same thing! Except they couldn't pull the Christmas lights down from the attic, thank God. So they went parading around our yard at night with flashlights and glow-sticks . . . Calling out and singing, 'I'm the Batman! I'm the Batman!'" She glances around, wide-eyed, as if to ask, Anyone else?

"Settin a bad example," James says again, mournfully this time. "I mean . . . Is this . . . all just some . . . stunt? Some . . . cry for attention?"

I give him a look, confused.

He scoffs at my silence. "Batman," he says, disgusted, and wags a finger at me. "You, sir . . . Are *no* superhero."

A rattle of sniggers clatters around the room. I square my shoulders and mutter just a little too loudly, "And yer no Jack Kennedy."

His face reddens purple and somehow Nora jumps all over me again before he can.

"Then..." she says. "Then my kids tell me you went and *told them where to get the LEDs!*" She reaches for her water bottle. "Why in the . . . bloody . . . hell . . . would you do such a thing?!"

Truth is, I have noticed kids calling me Batman and imitating me to some extent. Some even chant the *Batman* theme song, *Na-na-na-na-na-na* . . . But only a few. And as cool as it would be, it's not like I got all the kids in town all head-over-heels in love with bats.

I'm thinking there's no use sugar-coating the truth here. Being honest is not only the right thing to do, but I suspect it will also get me out of here more quickly. Good thing, too: My bats are hungry.

"Well . . . they're light bulbs," I say. "*Not* cigarettes. Not vape. Not drugs. Not even," and my mind goes completely blank as I attempt to come up with something else kids shouldn't be getting into. Part of not having kids of my own, I suppose. But then somehow, from somewhere beyond the two deep eyes cut into the dark of night by those naked window frames all the way across the room, it mercifully comes to me.

"*Porn.*" I sigh, and take a relieved breath, shaking my head. "So . . . Nuthin like that." I sigh again and smile weakly and look around the room and hope at least one other person sees my point. "What was I sposed to say to them?" I say. Silence. So I continue. "So there I am. Mindin my own business, walkin my bats, when some kids come runnin up and point at the spikes in my head and ask, 'Hey, where'd ya get the cool lights, mister?' Then all I say back is I bought em online." I scratch at the back of my neck and say, "Should I have lied to them instead?"

There's another silence my bats fill with a unified whispering of wings.

"Well of course not, Ned," Nora sighs. Her outstretched arms fall and slap against her hips. She looks at me and permits herself a small smile. After all, it's not like I've done anything wrong: I used to go for walks with my dog. He died. Now I walk with bats. Then I told some curious kids they sell lightbulbs on Amazon. That's it.

My bats swoop low, then break their large pinwheel rotation and settle upon a high joist, one after the other, forming a neat row like soldiers called to roll call.

"Do some reading!" Harriet rumbles. "These bats," she smacks, "are harmless."

I get up to leave, my Amazon-purchased LED bulbs tinkling.

"Bats schmats," I mutter, and think almost aloud, "Rabies schmabies." I make my way to the exit. I just recalled not missing this place much since I was here last.

I hesitate at the sight of my City Hall visitors from the other day standing in the old narthex. My LEDs clank softly as I send them a blank look. It had slipped my mind that they would be here tonight. My gaze lingers an extra half second before I move on. What am I supposed to do, I want to ask. Pull some sort of Pied Piper and march from town, the bats all trailing behind me to the next burg down the road?

I click on my LEDs and turn to leave the Great Room, the drab walls of the dim narthex twitching light blue and green. My bats streak out through the tall doors like black laser beams, scarcely clearing our heads.

"Ho-ly *hell*," I hear the older one say as the heavy doors thud shut behind me.

Night after night following the brutal attack on Jerome, during my slumber, that Jack Russell's teeth had pulled again and again from the deep meat of my hand. Night after night the dog thumping beneath the truck's tires, the snapping and popping crunches of its ribs, the horrible shrieking and dying whimper of my basset, and slurring-stroke-dude's head jerking around back and forth. But then in my nightmare the Jack Russell springs back up at me, half again its previous size. And out of reflex, I punt him back into the street, where he regathers, resizes himself by an additional one half, and comes charging back. Over and over I punt and re-punt the thing until it redoubles so many times it weighs more than I do, and soon it will have me and I keep pushing and trying to kick it away. Meanwhile, slurring-and-moaning-stroke-dude garbles louder and louder with each tear and thrash of the dog's claws ripping up my throat, until he finally moans so loud I wake up because it's actually me moaning—yelling, really—and clutching my throat, having pressed stinging tears from every pore of my flesh.

Then, shivering in the thick black of night, I'd reach for Jerome, and find only empty bed instead.

This had been a nightly vision until a bat followed me home from my evening walk through the UW-NC commons one night. The commons is relatively quiet during the summer session here, so the bat was easy to hear once it started chirping within earshot swoops, its ultrasonic speech weaving seamlessly into my thoughts, and mine into his. The bat kept its distance, sculpting the air as it continued to forage, and slyly noted I now walked the commons alone. Me, sans Jerome.

I pressed pus from the meaty flesh of my stiff and swollen hand, looking but failing to track the bat's impossible flight. On the third night, parting a prickly veil of mosquitos and gnats, the ambassador bat finally introduced itself.

Now, several months later, an enormous cloud of bats follows me around every night, these things called *my* bats, who so kindly offered me comfort, some solace, what with my dear Jerome buried beneath an arrangement of smooth stones out back and all.

Initially, I snorted at their offer, still unaffected by the fact I'd engaged in mental congress with this, a colony of the planet's one and only flying mammal, but nonetheless found myself unable to disagree. Not like I had a choice. Some things just come to you, and you have to learn to accept that. Artists learn with experience to let the art *come to them*. The trick is not to try too hard, not to force it. Let your subconscious take you. Embrace fugue. Open your paintings to darkness, your sculpture to shadow. Music to discord, and allow bent words into your verse.

Same with me and my bats. I didn't pick the bats. All of these bats, each and every one of them, picked me. And my nightmares stopped.

Now every night I step into something of a trance while walking my bats, slipping into a reverie of extraordinary comfort and well-being. It all begins while weaving a string of blue and green LED bulbs through the long spikes of my black hair. It's the sort of euphoria that often extends well beyond the walk itself, days when my little-blind-flying-mice musing blends into my workday, and while seated at my computer I catch myself tingling and numbed by the unified breathing of my sleeping bats back at my house, one hairy lung pressed to the joists in my attic, and I rock with the beating of hundreds of pink marbles drumming away back in their roost.

The LED lights, meanwhile, pull in insects which in turn draw the bats, and keep them tethered on beams of glowing gossamer threads as I tarry on my strolls, wandering city parks and walkways through the UW-NC grounds from dusk until midnight. Then again during the near-dawn, when I meander out to gather them in, bring them home. An invisible conduit conducts their chatter to my brains as they bustle overhead like a quivering cartoon thought bubble. Or sometimes my bats drift ahead, pulsating before me, a large dark sail bellied by the gentle Noisy Creek breezes, pulling me along, dipping and nipping across neighborhood seas, piercing dense insect and pollen plumes along the way.

After I return with my bats this morning, I recall that it's my turn at work to pick up treats from the bakery. There's a long line, so I wander over to inspect the doughnut case. Everyone inside is talking excitedly, the air electric. Like the day of a major election. Elspaith, the owner behind the counter, curves her slim frame around, flashing a broad smile. In a melodious but firm voice she says, "Bats are protected in Wisconsin."

"What?!" Homer exclaims. Of course he's here. Probably the one who started all this bat-yakking in the first place. Got some united front organized by now. Or a capital campaign complete with yard signs—BEES NOT BATS! or BATS: WINGS OF SATAN'S CHARIOT—and spinning up a GoFundMe page.

"Bats," Elspaith says, calmly boxing yet more delicate goodies. "Can't kill em." She looks down to insert a cardboard tab into a slot. She presses the box shut and, satisfied the lid will hold, looks back up. "Sorry to wreck your fun. Laws and such, ya know." She pauses for a moment to lock eyes with Homer, doing so in a way that makes me wonder what exactly Homer could have said before I walked in here. And even I catch a chill as her words now flow like a frozen river. "So don't even go there."

Elspaith rights her neck to adjust her gaze to a croissant-skinned older woman and slides the box across the counter. "Yer all set, then!" she sings, with an adoring smile.

"All bats?" Homer says, incredulous.

"*Any* species of bat in Wisconsin," Elspaith says. "Last summer a business coupla towns over got fined like eighty thou for fumigating the bats in their warehouse."

"I was reading about bats last night online, like Doctor Harriet said," Gail says. She works across the street at the insurance agency next to the hardware store. She places her order quickly and turns back to Homer. "They're *amazing*. Did you know that twenty-five percent of all mammals on Earth are bats?"

This is hard. Sounds as though Gail is on my side here, but she arrived by virtue of a bit of Google-fu. Though to her credit, she lacks the I've-known-this-all-my-life smugness you tend to see gush forth from people upon their acquisition of sudden expertise.

"No way," Homer says.

"Yep," Gail says. "It's on Britannica dot com and others. Mammals. Lions, tigers, bears. Voles, shrews, goats, and gophers. Whales and humans, too. Of all these, one in four's a bat."

Homer sinks into thought. I'm guessing he's considering becoming a sudden expert in his own right, possibly before his next coffee break, when at last he blurts, "What about vampire bats?"

Gail gathers her things. "Not to worry. Those all live south of the border. And they don't even suck human blood, anyway."

"Really," Homer says, underwhelmed.

"Yep." Gail turns to leave. "And I guess bats round here are super clean, too."

"Clean?"

"Rabies. Bats score really low on that. Like less than one-tenth of one-percent. Bats round here," she says, turning up a palm and smiling, "just eat bugs."

The line of customers edges forward a notch. It's almost Homer's turn to order. The bells on the door jangle as Gail pushes it open.

"Do some research," she calls out. "And just be happy spiders can't fly."

The rest of us can't help but grin, but Homer mutters, ominously, "Fine," and turns away from where Gail just departed. His face pales to an ashen green when he finally notices me. Homer folds his arms and narrows his eyes, engulfed by the sudden awareness of my presence here all this time.

"But we still need to do something," he says. "Some*thing* . . . must be done!"

All day long after I dropped off the treats in the break room at work, I could sense something off with my bats. Their distant breathing rubbed erratic, divided, and out of proper sync. And their hearts drummed and rippled in a disharmony of light-headedness. The sensation pulled and gnawed at me until now, when I finally return home to find my bats buzzing madly during tonight's reverie of insect nebulae, bat bubbles, and scattered bat kites. Black birthday balloon clusters tethered by rays of glimmering insect threads.

A stitching whisper throbs and envelops my consciousness, the bats' beams projecting a clear panoramic of a special session of the Noisy Creek City Council on the insides of my eyelids. There's Little Homer on the Prairie now, presenting a "thoroughly-researched" means of poisoning and killing all those darn bats he so adamantly wants to take a stand against, city smarties like Harriet, Elspaith, and Gail be damned.

Brent and James fade into view as my bloodied fingernails scratch at the relentless mosquitoes needle-pointing their way across my neck and shoulders. Turns out even my colony of ravenous bats can't eat them all. A rivulet of blood trickles down to an unreachable crevice between my shoulder blades, where it dries and itches. The bugs seem more bothersome tonight, wadding up in the corners of my eyes, droning in my ears, and needling up my nostrils. But I can still see Brent's adamant agreement with Homer, to which Council concurs by way of what looks like an off-the-books vote on an unofficial measure. The last glimpse I get of the scene as I cross the daunting Noisy Creek swinging bridge is that of Dr. Harriet Boslem storming out, calling Council's process "fraught with peril."

It's a surreal scene from a yet-to-be written dystopia. Harriet is gone. Council members with slick skin and heavy brows snigger and elbow and yuk and nod. The dim light inside is filtered smoke green. A box of stogies circles the room. The bats buzz fast. So fast it's impossible to follow the flurry of imagery and their chatter. Particularly above the roar of the aptly named Noisy Creek swaying beneath my feet. Dizzying glints of rapids flash thirty feet below through rot spots in the bridge boards tilting side to side. And it occurs to me my bats are about to do something drastic. That they intend to leave me. Here. In this town, with these people. Alone.

That was last night. When I finally went to bed, I dreamt that when I got up for my pre-dawn *murciélago* meandering,

I opened the door and was immediately flattened by a thundering torrent of bats. A black bat blizzard doing what my mother had warned me about mice as a child: They'll all run inside if you leave the door open too long. They're out there . . . lurking and waiting for you to drop your guard. Entire families of the things. Oh, my mother was terrified of the mice running into the house. And I'd imagine a mommy mouse, a daddy mouse, and five or six pinkies crouched in Mom's garden, peering over the edge of a boulder, lying in wait for me to dawdle carelessly at the door knob only to have the entire family scurry inside behind my back, overnight bags trailing in hand.

These are my bats, though, that flattened me so soundly. When I dust myself off and look up, I see hundreds swirling in a tight vortex above a beautiful woman, seated in a Naugahyde chair in the corner across the room behind me. Her hands rest on her lap and her eyes glisten deep and black, with white legs bare beneath the hem of a dark green dress and crossed at the ankles. The bat vortex tightens and my flesh pops and ripples with the rapid beating of thousands of pink marble-sized hearts, piano hammers drumming ever faster one layer beneath my skin.

"My darling," she says. "You must remember to keep your doors locked! . . . Always." She throws back her head and caws like a laughing raven, once, twice, and again and again, gradually quieter as she disintegrates into flakes of black bats peeling and fluttering up and away from her body. First her hair, then her eyes, all of her head disappears, one set of wings at a time, until she vanishes completely, shoulders down to shoes, a trail of black ashes sucked into the speeding bat vortex. I reach for her, but she's entirely gone. Gone into the black. There's just a chair, and one of her shoes. I drift away, pulled backwards out my kitchen door, coughing between two cubicles as I round someone's desk at work. Some guy whose name I never seem to get right, even when he wears a name tag to company picnics: Ben. Burt. Bert. Bryant. Byron. Brian. Brad. B something—a B name. Not Bob.

A few steps later, I'm outside after work and headed over to the Community Center to crash Council's special session "for the general public" to confirm their "final solution" when my bats cut me off halfway, throwing up a pulsating black wall. They swirl frantically about my head, some forming the familiar thought bubbles, others smallish dark sails to tug me away. Ambassador Bat informs me it's time to go. Go, as in away.

Right now, he tells me. Now, because it's already started: the ER at the UW-NC Medical Center is packed with sick kids and teachers who consumed a chemical that was introduced into a creekside backwater near the public school. The bats could easily detect the toxin, and avoided it. The people could not and did not. And now they're all dying. Meanwhile, the bats, the intended target, are still flying around same as before.

And on this mid-September night the bats—*my* bats— pack it in. The retelling and rebroadcast of local events that pour into my head from hundreds of dizzying signals sicken my heart. And it doesn't stop. Continuous beams of high-frequency versions of the same story: Systematic poisoning. Been the idea all along, the bats tell me. After the backwaters, the stagnant pools left behind the high school after last week's prolonged rainfall. Then any other standing water in the yards around the neighborhood: old car tires, overturned hubcaps, garbage cans and lids, frisbees, and so on. And now it's cascading out of control far beyond the bats.

These are my people. What have they done? What have they become?

My arms and legs hang heavy and drained and I want to throw up and plow myself in.

I shuffle through a curtain of cold, the woman from my dream who called me darling coming in to view, shining and gradually taking form, one bat at a time. A dozen bats swoop and coil into a tight spiral close around my head again, wings brushing my face, steering me. I murmur, "Who...?"

Time to go-*ooooh*, my bats sing. It's the whispering chorus of hundreds of swishing voices, that bellied sail straining before me, guiding me from town.

The night smells of musky trails and dewed grasses and welcoming cold. The drumming piano hammers from my dream fire up again and tingle beneath my skin and travel up my arms, ripple over my shoulders, coil in my back, and grasp my spine. "Where..." I ask. Me, led away by the bats I lead around, tethered fast by a pulsating stream of quavering insects. Me, leaving this town in their embrace, shivering in a shawl not of bravery but merely a lack of fear.

The cold deepens. Noisy Creek disintegrates behind me. Chilled leaves fold into damp sky. A tall copse of spruce, and a thicket of birch close around the dwindling path below.

My little blind flying mice. Some nights they fill the sky and blacken the moon, though tonight I remember only wet stars, larger and larger.

Boydlehook

Life for me in Boydlehook began starting at around age twelve. Before that, I hold few early childhood memories.

One is of a knothole in the fence with some kid's eye always watching, always peering into our yard, always on me.

Another is of fishing. Dad took my brothers and me fishing for trout once, twice, maybe three times, I think. He'd take us out and about, mostly to give Mom space. We didn't mind getting away, either, though each time ended in a hopeless tangle of monofilament, worm guts, and a flurry of Dad's red-faced expletives we were meant to pretend not to hear. Fishing was a lot like most excursions with my father, and always concluded with us attempting to sit still around a greasy table at some diner that still served beer. We'd glance down at our forks with dread, and imagine the clumsy, happy family who'd come before us, chins glistening bright yellow with warm, runny egg yolks. And the dishwashing machine back there, somewhere in the kitchen, a massive earthen kiln firing away, glazing the happy shiny chin people's egg yolk remains directly to the steep banks of the fork tine valleys we now held in our hands. We'd look around at the plaques and antlers screwed into the walls, the lacquered Green Bay Packer clocks, and the mummified forks and knives set out upon the bare tables dotting the tiled floor, while Dad drummed his fingers, and sighed, avoiding Mom and waiting for his can of Schlitz.

The unyielding eye next door, and the kid it belonged to, moved away from Boydlehook about a year after our last fishing trip. The eye was gone, but the hole remained. Dad was glad he moved, said that kid's special kind of stupid was probably catching, and that really worried him.

Then there was my uncle, who died very young. Dad said he was up in heaven now. Made him happy—gave him comfort, he said—to imagine his brother, tramping around, hunting deer somewhere up there. I looked at my father, murmuring in earnest and solemn reverie, and I could tell by his eyebrows, all tight and close together, and the curved shape his lips made, that I should be happy for my young dead uncle, too. But I wasn't. Hearing about him just made me queasy. All those fresh, warm gut piles spilled on the soils of paradise. Pile after pile delivered by a man far too young dead, heap after steaming heap of fresh deer guts. One, then another, strung together like connect-the-dots dots along the edge of a forest, disappearing into the beyond of some chilly morning in the afterlife.

The Butcher's Ghost

Bluffworld

A steep staircase rises next to the void where Sixth Street vanishes into the base of the bluff. Black granite steps jut from the earth like flats and sharps on a piano keyboard. In summer there are mosquitos and lush ivies. In fall, wet leaves. There are worms and birds in the spring, and in winter frozen mist crystals sparkle and coil overhead.

The stairs go up.

At the top of the stairs rests The Butcher's Ghost, a bar and restaurant built upon the burned-out ruins of Meat the Bluffs, a meat market in which the owner, Earl Fekete, lost his life in the same fire that claimed his market. Police investigators believe Mr. Fekete fell asleep on a cot in a basement storeroom shortly before the blaze engulfed the building. His remains were nearly entirely incinerated.

For more than a decade, the stone foundation lay bare and exposed, like an open grave, grown over and bearded with mosses and brambles, until a pair of honeymooning newlyweds were struck, while passing through, with the romantic vision of raising from the ruins a cozy neighborhood café.

There's no denying a certain magic and intrigue about the locale and its transformation today. The restored building, the granite staircase, the street that comes to an unexpected end at the base of a sheer three-hundred-foot cliff.

The world above the mist exists as an elevated island-town perched above the community below. A narrow cobblestone street winds through a tight residential neighborhood dotted by a small grocery store, a flower shop, a barber, a chocolatier, a cigar shop, a watchmaker, a bookseller, and The Butcher's Ghost—a bistro bar and café that is neither German beer hall nor Napa wine bar but something of each.

Down below, the yards and lawns at the end of Sixth Street ease into the bluff. One yard in particular is part bluff, grass trimmed and groomed, complete with tiers of elegant flower boxes planted thirty feet up the side slope. To the north, a fire pit where school children throw a party on the last day of school. They drink sparkling cider and roast marshmallows and toss their workbooks onto a hungry fire. The students belch and cheer. The fire hisses and snaps.

Why does the man climb the stairs?

Sunset over the far-off big city blushes purple and rose of bruised winter belly flesh. Oblong clouds roll and lumber on the horizon like waking gods. Middle-aged Dan and middle-aged Jim stand side by side in expensive business suits and look out the tall windows of their office building.

Wow, Dan thinks.

Gorgeous, Jim says.

Dan and Jim both nod. Jesus, Jim says. Dan continues to stare. His throat is cold and dry.

Dan uncrosses his arms and lets them hang at his sides. His left hand brushes the back of Jim's right.

Dan recoils and starts to shake his head when he sees Jim looking straight at him. Jim's eyes fill. Dan's eyes sparkle.

Dan sobs and nods on Jim's shoulder and Jim heaves and weeps snot into his fist.

Dan drifts away and stares. Jim shudders and finds his coat and takes his wife out for steak and chops and then later on back home to their paneled basement for missionary sex on a Naugahyde couch.

Dan goes home, too. Dan lives alone on Sixth Street one block away from the base of the bluff. He opens a bottle of beer and sits on his front steps. It's cold outside.

Dan's not from here, but he's adapted well. He likes to keep his family at a good distance, like the people here do. Not a close family that's constantly over for dinner and in your face like down in Chicago or out in Philly. Meals shared in suffocating silence, the loaded subtext of The Holidays, and insular aunts and uncles, terrified of difference. No, for Dan, right here, a half continent away, is close enough.

He tips the beer into his mouth and smiles and swallows and waves at a neighbor walking his dog. Dan has no idea who they are. The man and dog breathe in rhythm. Hot vapor escapes their mouths in synchronized chuffs. Dan takes a long drink of the beer and places the bottle into the snowbank and makes his way down Sixth Street to the place where the street becomes bluff. Dan feels there should be a tunnel here. If he were to continue along the street, he'd pass straight through the wall into a world enclosed within the bluff. Like Platform 9¾. You just have to believe it's there, and if there's enough cosmos in your blood, an apocryphal aperture will draw you in. Swallow you up. Like Jim's shuddering hug.

Dan wants another sip of the beer he shoved into the snowbank back at his house. It's starting to get very cold. His expensive business suit isn't very warm. He is drawn to the top of the long staircase like smoke up a chimney. The snow is deep. It takes a while.

The planet spins. Do we?

Mother died minutes ago. Finally. Janet pulls her car to the side of the street. Her brain flows, awash in muffled gusts of underwater swimming noises. It's the sound of cold gelatin pressed into your ears. She drops her car into Park on the narrow cobblestone street on top of the bluff. She needs to call her brother, Randy.

Janet looks out her car window and scans the parking lot behind The Butcher's Ghost. A lamp above the doorway beneath the sign casts a cone of light onto the dark landing where a man opens and holds the heavy wooden door for a woman. She steps through the doorway and shakes her hair. The man follows her inside, stomping snow from his boots in the foyer. Janet turns her attention back to her brother.

But not yet. She needs to eat something first. She glances at The Butcher's Ghost again, then at her phone. Randy will answer first ring. Beer would be good, too. Randy is a pain in the ass.

She keeps killing me

Cable television news rants ranting rants around the neighborhood. But much to Dan's relief, there is no television set here at The Butcher's Ghost. A bar in the Upper Midwest with no television screens. Somehow. No red-faced sportscasters, no millionaire college dropouts chasing balls around, no springy homecoming royalty reading aloud the weather forecast or sharing dieting tips.

Just a scattered copy here and there of the local *Vulpine Valley View*, always folded open at the daily crossword puzzle.

Dan stares at the menu, the stylized entrée sections. *Shared Plates. Rabbit Food. Land and Land. Rivers and Lakes.* Will he order something? Entrée or à la carte? He fell in love with this place when he first moved to town and discovered the black steps, the absence of electronic screens. Not even a cellphone lit up in here, no eerily glowing and detached faces. Just the tactile attachment of human eye contact. Now Dan can hardly stay away.

But Dan realizes that apart from all else, it's Fekete's messages that draw him in. Beneath the final menu entry reads an always-haunting and enigmatic note. A vignette, almost. A random chip thrown at a mosaic on the wall, attempting to tell a larger story. The first time it read *What did you do last night? I caught on fire.* Then the next night, *How many times can you kill a ghost?*

The message is always different. *Burned alive. Beneath your feet.* Last time Dan was here it read, *I smelled perfume, drank whiskey, and ate flames.* That one stayed with him all the way down through the icy mists of the slippery granite stairs, past the smell of the charred stones at the kids' fire pit, all the way home, all the way into his kitchen where he sat alone, like the butcher burned in the bluffs, all by himself. Those messages that now constantly ring in his head. A ringing whisper . . . *and ate flames.*

Who kept killing Fekete? Dan remembers little else of the *ate-flames* night. Just a lack of appetite, his kitchen, a shape moving outside his kitchen window that disappeared when he stood up, and a powerful funneling feeling with nowhere to flow.

Or, or, or, or or

Either no one else but Dan notices or no one else can read, which is why no one else mentions the ever-changing and haunted menu messages. *She only wanted my gold fillings.* Or they notice and they don't care. Or maybe they do notice but they're too scared to care or to say anything. *Hung on a hook and left to roast.* Or maybe no one knows how those messages truly get there. *I was still wearing my butcher boots.* Or they just ignore it all. All of everything.

Or it's something else. *Burned my skull and poured out my melted fillings.* Maybe they notice and they know exactly how the messages get in the menu and where they come from. And they know what it all means. Or they do know, but they don't know what to do with what they know. Or maybe it's all about nothing or maybe it's only Dan who sees the messages. Visible only to him. *Always the same flames.* Or something.

Did I...?

Janet steps inside The Butcher's Ghost and shakes off the cold. She seats herself at a bar stool and orders a black beer and asks for a menu. Beside her, two men resume a conversation they paused in order to watch her twist free of her long coat.

Good people, then?

What?

The people yer workin with. Are they—

Oh. Ja. I mean . . . They're alright, I guess.

Janet orders a Boyfriend Portion of braised beef tenderloin tips and horseradish and a side of American fries. She coughs and slides the newspaper before her and scans the crossword puzzle and pulls out a pen and completes 4-down all in one motion.

There should be a tunnel

Dan watches the man seated across the dining room finish his meal. *The troubles above us . . . Darker than the new moon.* The red wine looks good. The man wipes the corners of his mouth with a dark linen napkin, then pulls the cloth through each pair of fingers. He drops the cloth onto his plate and folds his hands and looks around for his server. The man's gaze grazes the bar area. Dan looks down at his menu. *You have more to fear from the living than the dead.* The man rises and walks around his table to ease out the chair for a woman seated beside him. He takes her hand. She stands and presses a palm onto the man's chest and tilts her head up to the man. The man catches Dan's eye and holds his gaze for an extra moment until the man turns his head to the woman to kiss her on the mouth. It's a long kiss. The man is middle-aged Jim, who earlier watched the waking-god-clouds at sunset next to Dan. Middle-aged Jim strides out of the restaurant with the woman Dan presumes to be middle-aged Jim's wife. Middle-aged Jim nods knowingly to the hostess. Dan turns his head away. He thinks he smells an overripe something coming from the basement.

She keeps killing me.

Corcovado has a teleférico

Dan glides down the staircase of black sharps and flats. Feels like threading an airplane between high walls of a narrow runway carved into a dense forest. Treetops slip overhead like layers of sea. Dan clutches for the railing in a semi-controlled float. The stars and moon are cold and bright and damp.

By now, Dan has mastered the winter stairs. *She tried to push me down The Black Steps once.* But he still feels dizzy and light in the stomach. *Make it look like I slipped.* He longs for an appetite. *I never slipped.* He longs to long. *Ever.* He's longed for so long.

Hot dog!

Janet looks from her black beer at the bar to the local newspaper again, opened to the daily crossword puzzle. 9-across: *Dammit, _____. (Rocky Horror damsel.)*

She mutters a profanity.

The man next to her turns his head. What is it, he asks. She can tell he's been dying to say something to her anyway.

Janet sighs. This, she says. She pulls her dark black bangs aside and drops a fingertip onto the clue for nine-across. The man reads and instantly a bright smile parts his beard.

Janet! he calls out, quietly.

Janet's clear brown eyes go cold. He ceases what he was about to start.

What?

My name is Janet, she says. Her eyes soften. Slightly. He raises his chin and inhales slowly through his nostrils. He returns to his friend.

Janet waits for her food. The man will say nothing more about *Rocky Horror.* Not to her, not tonight. She looks back at the crossword puzzle. She reads more clues and stops at 16-across and looks toward the window where the bluff plummets. She can only see the small dining area reflected back at her in sepia. Janet pushes her empty beer glass towards the edge of the bar and nods to the bartender and looks back at the crossword puzzle. 16-across is a long one.

A kid'll eat ivy, too

At the base of the Sixth Street steps, Dan stares at the side of the bluff again. It is very dark, but the glittering moonlit mist reflects the granite layers in the bluff where the tunnel should open. He smells the memory of last spring's fire-pit embers, the surrounding air crisp with sparkling-cider ghosts of parties past.

The temperature has dropped, and Dan needs to keep moving. *There was no other way out.* The bluff is solid rock and there was nowhere for the butcher burned in the bluffs to go once the fire began to rage. Maybe the butcher was burned *into* the bluffs. Maybe there was a tunnel, but the fire closed it off with him in it. Maybe. *The living. Fear the living. Not the dead.*

In his mind, Dan refers to this spot as the *tunnel entrance* even though there is neither a tunnel nor an entrance. His longing penetrates the solid granite, presses onto the packed walls that don't exist, and detects a whiff of a moist dirt trail mirage beyond. But there is only solid granite and the beginning of those sharp black stairs.

Dan decides that Spring will bring back the vines and ivies as well as a portal. A secret crevice, a divide, a window, a door, a crack that forms an arch, a hole. Anything, really. Something that will appear beneath a new and verdant growth. But for now, there is nothing. Nowhere for anything but for Dan to flow.

Straight down is straight down

Janet finishes her Boyfriend Portion and black beer and pushes away from the bar. She wraps herself in her long jacket and nods to the men next to her and walks out. She passes a table of elderly diners. They were there when she came in.

A woman speaks. Is this mint, she asks. Her cheeks are bright red, like apples. They move a lot when she talks. Janet turns her head toward the source of the woman's voice. Reminds her of a corkscrew twisting into a very dry cork. The woman lifts a limp green leaf from a plate of strawberries.

I'd sniff it to find out, the woman says. But my nose'd drip.

Something about how dripping-nose-woman's shoulders move reminds Janet of her mother who died not two hours ago. Then a memory of a spontaneous game of parents-versus-kids softball Janet and her friends started up while on a group picnic at an intramural field during an unexpectedly pleasant May afternoon. Children shrieked as moms and dads took the field. All but Janet's mother. Mom stood frozen behind the home plate backstop, an old mom. And fat. A ball glove dangled from a wide fingertip. Janet's panic hung frozen mid-air between the dugout and pitcher's mound. Finally, her mother leaned against a tree, resigned, and crossed her legs at the ankles.

A cascade of sorrow and relief leveled Janet. It was a terrible moment. A line-drive shot past her into right field while staring at her mother staring at her, jaw unhinged and swung open, someone else's clumsy mitt swaying uselessly from the tips of her fat fingers.

A man's voice fast-forwards Janet back to The Butcher's Ghost. His throat rattles tell-tale of a daily lush.

Absurd, he scoffs. The man continues a slurred rant about the First Family.

Janet steps out into the dark cold and walks past her car to the edge of the bluff. She looks across the flat expanse of silent treetops toward the horizon. Janet loves this view. It is beautiful. A stubborn thin mist woven through the treetops glistens a vast silver moon pool. She peers over the precipice. She hears movement and spots amorphous dark shapes gliding through the woods below. She nods. Deer, probably. Or wolves. Across the treetops, random city lights flicker through bare limbs like hatching mayflies.

She turns toward her car and remembers the woman in the restaurant, the mint leaf. A plate of fresh strawberries this time of year, Janet thinks. She sniffs the black air. She needs to call Randy. The amorphous dark shapes are gone. Janet blinks, tears frozen in the lash.

Ectoplasmosis

Dan returns to the house and plucks the beer bottle from where he inserted it into the snowbank. Approximately three ounces of partially frozen beer remain. *Oh, the reek of burned blood.* He sets the beer bottle on the kitchen counter and pours himself a glass of wine and sits down at the kitchen table. *I had to smell my own burning hair, too.* He opens the newspaper and performs a well-practiced crossword-puzzle fold on the crossword-puzzle page. *She's coming back.*

Sometimes he thinks he hears someone outside. Like tonight. Usually, when he walks to the front room, there is nothing, whatever sounds outside choked and put down by the cold. Dan figures he's probably still getting used to this new place. The rhythms of the town, the knocks of the neighborhood, the pops and sighs of the old house. Tonight, though, there appears to be a shape outside. *Relax,* his older brother used to tell him. That fuzzy dark thing you thought you saw scurry across the floor? he'd say, every night, every stinking night, It's probably just a tarantula.

The shape enlarges as it approaches the front steps. Dan stands. He hears a key turn in the lock. Tarantulas don't have opposable thumbs. Dan doesn't recall locking the door. The shape steps through the door onto the mat in the entryway. Sharp air rushes in. The shape is a person. A woman, Dan can tell. Dan tries to speak, but words refuse to come out. The woman groans quietly as she turns out of her long coat. She pulls off her boots and clicks on a lamp.

She drops her keys and gloves on a familiar entryway table and strides into the house. Dan steps toward her and tries to speak. *Why do you keep haunting me?*

Janet doesn't react to Dan standing in the middle of her living room. She passes through Dan on the way to the kitchen. Dan turns. The beer bottle is gone. The wine glass is gone. The newspaper rests on the kitchen table, undisturbed. Janet opens the refrigerator and removes a chilled glass of water and sits down.

Dan glides into the kitchen. He wants to say something. Something like, It's very late, ya know, but Janet sits down and opens the *Vulpine Valley View* to the crossword. Dan stands beside Janet, watching. It's what he does. Makes him feel a little less dead. She completes the puzzle until she arrives at 16-across. She looks in Dan's direction out the window toward the bluff beyond. Dan nods. Janet murmurs. 16-across is a long one.

Yard Mary

Sometimes our moms took us along when they went to work for our dads on the other side of town, scrubbing toilets and folding underwear. That's how we learned about the Yard Marys, and the sacred Naming ritual.

Yard Marys sprouted from the lawns over there, one per yard. Most were made of porcelain or some kind of glass. Some grew from cement, and others were said to grow from plastic. I never saw one of those. But it didn't really matter. Our other-sisters' families were very proud, and they all submitted to their holy Yard Marys morning and night.

The Yard Marys eventually named the children born into the homes they watched over. Sometimes it took years. This surprised us at first because we thought something like a Naming would happen right away, like it did with us on this side of town: at birth.

These other-sisters' Marys gave them beautiful names like Delilah and Penelope and Basimah and Jamila. On this side of town, our moms gave us names like Gert and Donda and Bobbalee and Dot. I'm Dot. Mom says it's short for Dorothy, but everyone calls me Dot.

My other-sisters lay on their backs at the feet of their Yard Mary as the sun rose and the sun set to wait for her to drop tears. My dad said that when the tears flowed, they always flowed black. Black as ravens, he said. Black as ravens disappearing into the night of the mouths of their babes.

I asked my dad if he'd ever seen a Yard Mary cry. He said no, but he shook his head in awe just the same.

Our other-sisters told us how the Yard Marys' tears alit on the tongues of the faithful, landing with a whisper that spoke to them their given Yard Mary name. They'd stick out their tongues, showing off the special black spots where the black kisses of their Yard Marys' tears landed. They strutted around, all snotty and superior, fresh alabaster skin aglow, whenever we visited with our moms.

Until then, the other-sisters' skin seemed pale, their eyes deep and sunken with dark streaks beneath. I think the Name-waiting kept them awake all night. Or maybe it was the fear of ending up a Never-named. It was hard to know.

There were no Marys in the yards on our side of town. Instead, we had spindly trees and houses that flaked paint. The trees bore no fruit but rather were thick with plastic shopping bags that rattled in the top branches. A plastic-bag ceiling that darkened our yards year-round. Older bags gathered rainfall and dew that leaked a constant dingy drizzle during the warmer months. Theses bulging bags turned to solid blocks of ice in the winter, and snapped branches when the wind blew hard. The frozen bags came down like anvils. And the paint chips gusted around the yards in coils like leaves in the fall.

The trees were put here to snag the plastic shopping bags before they could blow out into the ocean.

None of us had ever seen the ocean. A man from The City came by before all the tree-planting started and showed photos of water and an endless wad of plastic floating on top. He moved the tip of his finger slowly to show which was the ocean, and which was the plastic. His fingertip rested on the image of the "plastic-bag barge" he said was already twice the size of Texas.

"Three times France!" one of the men wearing a dark suit next to him said. He looked at each one of us to make sure we all heard. He seemed pretty excited, like someone does when they're telling a juicy secret.

He pointed at a pamphlet in his hand. OUR YARDS, OUR OCEANS. It was up to us, the OYOO pamphlet read, to provide the last line of defense for the oceans. The trees would keep the oceans clean and would work like a huge collection of dream-catchers. Except that these trees would catch plastic shopping bags instead of the things we would dream about.

"Gotta save the oceans," he said, and handed me the pamphlet and walked away, shaking his head. I looked down the street. I turned the pamphlet over. There was an American flag on the back. I looked up again. Paint chips tumbled on the lawn between me and another man on the sidewalk. That man nailed a OYOO poster onto a telephone pole over a hand-made LOST CAT sign. I heard him tell someone else that by letting The City dig up our lawns, we were doing our part. That what we were doing out here, hundreds of miles from everywhere, was heroic.

I asked a man digging holes in our yard where the bags came from. Maybe we could stop the bags before they started to fly around? Maybe cut down on all this digging? There were so many holes.

"The overflowing landfills," he said. "Over time, the bags rise, one by one, from the landfills."

"Plastic-bag zombies," I murmured, and imagined a squadron of flying un-dead coming for our brains, but getting snagged in the treetops at the very last second, right before they could get us. I looked up at the trees again. A bag flapped back at me.

Summer pressed on. I wondered about my dad's other children across town, and why they got to have Yard Marys and we didn't. After all, we had the same dad. They had a lot of things that we didn't, and I didn't say anything, really. Though I did want a Yard Mary. I think we all did, despite them being so creepy. I think it was the power of a Yard Mary growing and pushing up through the humus, strong and deliberate like a mushroom. First the cap, then the silky gilled veil that flapped over the soft skin of her face, and finally her shoulders that flexed and shrugged when the weather changed. And of course, those eyes. Clear eyes that always seemed to stare just over your head and convince the unnamed children under her watch to stay pure, and submit to her, morning and night.

My sisters and I looked down and scratched at the ground with our toes when a named Yard Mary sister strutted by, skin radiant. Spotted tongue hanging out all proud. I'm pretty sure I hated them. Probably hate. Hate is an easy thing when it comes to family.

That said, I don't think the other-sisters had a reason to hate any of us, though. They were pretty quiet about it if they did. Probably because we didn't look up to our bag-trees for anything special the way they looked up at their Yard Marys. Our parents gave us these basic names when we were born, and we lived beneath gangly trees that collected garbage. What was so special about that? Couldn't compare to their Naming ritual, those magical black drops that dripped so warmly into their mouths. It was a cosmic delivery with a divine name captured within, and together we on this side of town longed for our tattered shopping bags, swinging and rattling high above us, to mean more.

One hot day in August, I asked the man leaning on a shovel why they didn't dig up the parking lot at the empty strip mall behind our house, and just plant the bag-catching trees there instead.

"Way more space," I said. I thought about the boarded-up storefronts, the broken blacktop, the tall weeds shooting up through the cracks, and the rusty shopping carts stacked all over the place.

"Can't," he said. "Owner says he's got a buyer." He rested his shovel handle against a shoulder. "Some new church goin in there," he said. "And ya know they'll prolly need that parking." He paused to scoop dirt. "Until then," he said, and cut into the soil, "the owner's lettin the homeless sleep under them shopping carts out in the lot."

I didn't say anything. We had a lot of churches in my town.

Why couldn't I have a Yard Mary? Why did I need to live beneath a lake of dripping shopping bags? Were my shopping bags pretty, and loaded with secrets, and I was simply unable to see it?

I climbed a tree to find out. Discover the bags' secret. I insisted in my own mind that a divine magic trembled within them in the same way that some power I couldn't put my finger on allowed the trees to catch the bags in the first place. That the bags were our version of plastic-fleshed Yard Marys.

My father pulled me down the first time. He was never around much, so I wasn't exactly expecting to see him. I hid my reddening face by bending over to smooth my skirt with the palms of my hands and rub a scrape on my shin. He folded his arms and reared back and said that's no way for a young woman to behave, climbing trees.

His mouth became a straight line. "And do something about all these damn paint chips," he said, and waved his arms around. He climbed into his shiny car, looked at me, then at the house, and back at me, lips still a straight line, and drove away, shaking his head.

The worker in charge of planting more bag-trees watched my dad drive away. He looked at me sadly, and said that I may as well just leave the bags up in the branches.

"But they block the sun," I said, and pointed up. "And they're ugly." I wrinkled my nose at the man.

Just then a cluster clattered.

The man shrugged and yelled, "What?"

"Ugly!" I hollered. "Loud, too," I said, and raised my arms. "Always rattling. Like tambourines!"

I could tell he didn't disagree. But he said that no matter what I did with the plastic shopping bags after I took them down, they'd one day make their way to the landfill. And the landfill was plugged, so the bags would rise again, and take flight and head out to the ocean.

It seemed that stopping the bags was as futile as attempting to stop bad weather. I closed my eyes. Instead of plastic-bag zombies, images of a slurry of shopping-bag salmon flowed, mindlessly leaping upstream against the current to migrate and reproduce, and one day inevitably merge with that ever-swelling Triple-France at sea.

The Yard Mary children never seemed to worry about all the plastic bags. Maybe it was because they didn't have bag-trees growing in their yards.

Instead, my other-sisters seemed more concerned with making sure we knew about where they came from and those cool dots on their tongues. I thought the dots looked like some kind of tongue fungus, but they were all proud and smug.

"How many dots do you got, Dot?"

"Dot's got no dots!"

"Dotless Dot."

"No-spotty Dotty."

And so on, oh so clever. They were so certain, yet so desperate. The black liquid touch of the Yard Marys gave them what they wanted but made them more needy. More empty, maybe? I don't know. I mean, their years of prayers had been answered. They'd been Mary-named. Why weren't they happier?

One day, an unfrozen bag hit the ground. I was seated crisscross applesauce on our front lawn, using threads of dried grasses to tie small sticks into an octagon—I liked octagons—when I sensed the thud behind me. There was only a pressing, not a sound. A soundless *whoosh* of dead water hitting soft soil that breathed across my back. I turned my head and pulled my bangs aside. The gray mass lay not ten feet away, a flat wobbling bulge. I walked over to the bag, stick-work in hand.

The bag hadn't burst.

"Maybe it's like a Yard Mary," I whispered to my sticktagon. "Yard Marys don't leak, either." I watched the bag's last wobbles subside. "Except . . . when they give a Name." I tilted my head to a side. The man near the street hopped up on a shovel to start another hole. I folded my arms and looked at the squares of faded green paint peeling from the side of our house. I sighed. Maybe this bag would give a name, too, once it leaked. I turned the sticktagon over in my hand and looked up, wondering how many other bags were about to fall to the ground. The house flaked more paint. Bags would continue to fall, like October apples. Maybe a Mary in our yard could set all this mess straight.

I lifted the bag carefully by one of its plastic loop handles. The bag spun slowly before me, at arm's length, quivering like a swollen bladder. The water inside swished dingy and tinged. Then it twisted back in the opposite direction, the round yellow Walmart smiley-face considering me in gradual panoramic reveal. The bag dangled from my fingertips. How did this thing not lose any water?

More bags landed silently the next day. I looked up from where I was raking paint chips to ask one of the men planting bag-trees what to do with them.

"Pick em up for sure," he said, and glanced around the yard. He frowned at all the paint chips. "Then try to re-use em. Somehow." He started to walk away—sometimes I got the feeling that I was bothering him—but he quickly added, "Empty em first, of course . . . That water looks pretty nasty," he said, his voice rising way up at the end. He shuddered and grimaced and laughed.

I didn't say anything, but I agreed. I leaned the rake handle against my shoulder and turned the octagon-of-twigs over in my hands. It wasn't done yet. About seventy things that I could do with the bags popped into my mind.

"Maybe I'll build something with them," I said.

"Sure," the man said, and smiled. "Whatever you like. My wife uses em for sink garbage."

"Isn't that the same as sending them back to the landfill?"

"Well," the man said. "Yes. I suppose it is. But this way—"

"And from there won't they just fly around again? And then end up—"

"*This* way," the man said, and sighed loudly. "*This* way, you don't use up one of your mom's fresh, clean trash bags." He smiled like I've seen my dad smile when he explains something to my mom.

"My mom—"

Another bag landed on the soft ground behind the man. He jumped and blurted out, "But you do with them what you please."

I wandered over to pick up the bag that fell behind him, thinking about how bags boomerang around.

Even though I was building my own Yard Mary, I was never really sure if I believed in the Yard Mary magic. The whole Naming thing seemed like a lot to believe in. Just lying on the ground before the Yard Marys every sundown and every sun-up, mouth open, was a lot. I mean, how much worshipping did these Mary things need? But I guess hope is strong, and each of our other-sisters hoped for their Yard Mary to cry while they were laying there, flat on their backs, mouths agape. What if their Yard Mary cried while they were at school, or away playing? At a piano lesson?

"Violin," one of my other-sisters corrected.

"Harp," said another, lips sealing like a stitch.

Neither of them answered the question.

And why did the Yard Marys cry in the first place? I kept that question inside.

Fall was starting to age out. I continued to gather the occasional fallen tree bags and rake paint chips so my dad wouldn't yell at me again. Sometimes I nailed the paint chips back onto the side of our house. I tried nailing the neighbors' skin-colored chips that had blown into our yard back onto their house, but the dad came out and told me to stop it. Said he couldn't hear the game over my hammering. I asked if the hammering was any louder than the racket the overhead bags were making.

"WHAT?" he screamed, frowning as he put his hands on his hips and shook his head at me.

I did what he said. His chips kept splitting and breaking under the nails anyway.

Sometimes I raked our paint chips into a fallen tree bag, and other times I just raked them into a pile and my sisters and I would jump into them over and over again. It was fun. We watched a circle of men smoke and chat and stand around one man jabbing a shovel at a hole. Maybe the Yard Marys cried because of the bag-trees, and why we needed them. But that didn't make sense, either. Then why only give Names if that's what they were sad about? We threw paint chips up over our heads. Years of Yard Mary rituals and all our town got out of it was some snotty kids with cool names? The flakes drifted back down around us like confetti. None of this made any sense. Some of the flakes stuck to our skin.

My other-sisters went to a different school on the other side of town. But one of them went to mine. I think it was because she wasn't Named yet. She was tell-tale pale, and sad every morning until recess. It was only when she ran around and played games that she ever seemed kinda happy. I thought about how her skin would glow once she got her Name, once her Yard Mary cried into her mouth, and her

Yard-Mary Name would land with a whisper and dye her tongue with a swirl of black dots. And I'd be happy for her.

She'd strut all day long with her glowing skin and her tongue out and Teacher would tell her all day long to put it back. She'd fold her arms across her chest and roll her eyes and I'd go back to hating her. Until then, we had to witness her daily dread.

I told her about the plastic-bag Mary I was making in my yard. She spun away and left. I thought she was angry, or offended, maybe.

Or maybe she felt it absurd. Me, believing that a hand-made Yard Mary would actually work. I could picture the shape her face would make as she rolled her eyes and muttered *As if.* Or maybe she was embarrassed for me that I couldn't see what a stupid idea the whole bag-Mary thing was.

I raked paint chips for a while, listened to the men's shovels scrape the freezing earth, and worked with my sticktagon. And I realized that I would probably need a real Yard Mary. So, I set down my sticktagon and gathered some kids on my street and told them my plan.

That night, we snuck out of our homes and crept across town to where our other-sisters lived. We chose the darkest yard we could find. The air there was quiet and smelled of cold leaves and crisp grass. The shrubs lining the yard had straight edges that made long square shadows across the lawn under the moonlight. We brought along a shovel, a hand saw, a crowbar, a rope, and a burlap bag.

The Yard Mary's shoulders tensed when she saw us and our implements, but she continued to stare over our heads, like she didn't see us, as they tend to do. A beaded rosary dangled from her hands, pressed together in prayer.

We tried to pry up the Mary with the crowbar. We tied a rope around her neck and we all pulled together. We tried to dig her up with the shovel. We gritted our teeth and tried to push her over, and we even tried to saw her off at the ankles. I hacked and others shoved. But it was no use. She never flinched.

One of my sisters finally stopped yanking at her and simply asked the Yard Mary, basked in yellow moon-glow, if she'd like to come over to our side of town. We were already terrified after all that pulling and yanking and sawing, but when her mouth curled and popped open to speak . . . We all shrieked and ran away screaming.

My mom found the crowbar in the yard the next morning when she went over to clean. She gave me a look and sucked her teeth when she put the crowbar away in Dad's toolbox. She never said a thing. But she knew.

We never said so, but I think we all decided against trying to steal another Yard Mary after that. I pictured growing beneath her an intricate root system that intertwined with the underground branches of the oaks, cottonwoods, and elms, and even all that plumbing and storm-sewer network down below. Part of the earth. Plus, you're never the same once a thing like that thwarts you. Always second-guessing yourself. Though one time, when no one was looking, I kicked a Yard Mary as she was beginning to sprout, and leaned into another, just to see, but neither would budge. If anything, the bigger one pushed back.

A week or so later, about the time I'd already forgotten about our failed Yard Mary heist, the other-sister who went to my school—the one I told about my plastic-bag Mary— came by our house. I was working with another sticktagon. I was stunned by her visit, but knew she'd come for a reason.

A reason she didn't have to explain, either, the way her skin glowed. My other-sister had been Named!

I never thought this would happen. Part of me wanted to believe that they had been making the whole thing up. Another part of me was so happy for her. And the rest of me still hated her.

"She cried a lot this morning!" my other-sister said, choking up. She raised a clear jar and tilted it for me to see. A black fluid swished and sloshed inside. It cast a dark aura that absorbed the glow of her hands, her forearms seeming to end in stubs at the wrists.

"You didn't need to steal one, you know," she said. I didn't know what to say. Maybe being Named also meant you suddenly knew everything. I looked down at my shoes, trying not to notice all the paint chips.

"All you had to do was ask!" Her voice was exuberant. And other-otherly. Like it came from a place beside her but not a part of her. "You could have joined us!"

I blinked at her. Her eyes gleamed with an eerie sparkle.

"You're so pale," she said, with a pitying look. "Here." She unscrewed the lid and wiped her nose on the sleeve of her jacket. "You need a Name, too." A coil of steam rose from the jar. Her damp eyes gazed straight and far away through mine. "You do," she insisted, and pressed the jar into my hands.

I gasped and held the jar full of the thing I was certain didn't exist. I felt its warmth spread up my arms, and watched the black consume my palms. I swirled it around. It was as my dad had said: Black as ravens. The liquid quivered, eager to fly into the darkness of the night sky of my mouth.

"What name did she give you?" I whispered. I felt my voice shake.

"Drink and you tell me," my other-sister chirped.

Only an hour since her Mary cried away my other-sister's dread, and here she was right before me, forever smug. She glanced at my plastic-bag Yard Mary, rising up from a bed of arranged paint chips. Her yellow smiley Walmart face stretched out at us, straining with bag-tree fluids. Her veil made from window-washing rags flapped, and the strands of hair made from broken shoe laces taped to her head rose and fell. Her beer-bottle-cap rosary clattered in her clasped sticktagon hands, and the big black Walmart eye-dots on her round yellow face lifted and gazed over our heads indifferently.

I tipped the jar to my lips. A mouthful of tears. Black, thick, and viscous. The air was cold, but the fluid was still warm. And drier than I expected. It ran down my throat and scratched salty and metallic, more like blood than tears. But the flavor was much lighter, with a vanilla aftertaste that tickled. I wanted to drink more, but my other-sister pulled the jar away.

She started to say something, then stopped and stared at me with the intensity of someone who was seeing something new for the very first time.

"What is it?" I said.

She shook her head. A man cutting the earth open for another bag-tree stopped what he was doing. He rested against the long handle of his shovel, and watched.

I swallowed and exhaled. My tongue felt different. My Yard Mary of sticks and bags stirred again. Her rosary rattled. The man resting on his shovel tilted his head. A torn OYOO pamphlet tumbled and scraped along the sidewalk. Then the bag-tree canopy hushed for once, and the birds sang. I looked into my other-sister's eyes and opened my mouth and uttered her new Name.

Then I shook my head. Told her I didn't want the Name that the tears from the jar had just given me.

Her mouth flew open. "You can't reject it!" she shrieked, horrified. Truly horrified. Like my eyeballs had just been dug from their sockets with a spoon.

Something about her next shriek froze me. I couldn't move. She gasped again and extended a tentative fingertip to my cheek. It came back black. Black as ravens. She stared at her finger and raised her eyes to me hesitantly. My cheeks were wetter now, my boots fused to the Earth. My other-sister backed away. I flicked my eyes down and saw my boots stained black. Black spots from my black tears. She took another step backwards and screamed and ran away past the man resting on his shovel.

The raven-black tears streamed steadily down my face and onto my boots, waiting for someone's mouth to open, I think. Waiting. And crying. Because that's what Yard Marys do.

Oliebollen Destiny

The European baker in my hometown called them *oliebollen*. We called them donut holes. He considered them the bakery equivalent to cheese curds, and I thought of them as my only decent chance at being cool or popular my freshman year of high school.

My sort-of buddy, Kyle, always said not to worry, that I'd be fine. But that's not how I saw it. All my previous attempts at popularity only made me look desperate and needy, and it wasn't until later in the school year that I realized that this one would, too.

I'd skip first bell most every morning and hit Niemeijer's Bakery downtown rather than attend Typing class. I crossed the rocks of the small stream on the way to school, crouching and pausing in the cool Fall air to check for trout in the dark eddies near the Maple Street bridge. The bakery stood on the other side of the high riverbank, the crumbling brick high school two blocks up the street behind me where Maple crossed Grove. Sometimes I hesitated—maybe I shouldn't skip class?—but reminders of what awaited me in Mr. G's classroom—endless typing and retyping of *The organ grinder has a monkey*—made hitting Niemeijer's the obvious choice.

The purpose of the oliebollen trek was thus two-fold. While on the one hand it spared me Mr. G's morning monkey mania, it more importantly allowed me to snag some treats for the cool guys I was desperate to become friends with, as well as get close to the girls in the hot-chick clique with whom those guys flirted. And I was convinced that that sweet, same-day bakery freshness in my bag . . . could be capable of overpowering the stink of my dismal social standing.

My offerings were well received, though not without a certain awkwardness and hesitation. Should Kelli be seen talking to me? And Anna? Things like that. Some would pluck a steaming wad from my bag and pop it into their mouth and spin away, long hair swishing around like a cape, all in one motion.

Joelle, though, was different. I didn't really know her very well before ninth grade, but I did know that one thing we had in common was being undersized. While our classmates slinked and strutted around in bodies of adult proportions, Joelle and I were relegated to the unpopular crowd of ninth-graders referred to unflatteringly as "late bloomers." Joelle acted as though she didn't care. But she did. We all did.

Joelle was also the smartest person I knew. Clever, darting, shining black eyes, Joelle always had something to say.

"Yer such an asshole," she said one day, standing next to me and snatching another treat from my greasy white bag. She pressed the doughy lump between her moist lips and bit one half of it. Her puckered lips formed a perfect glazed heart as she chewed and smirked, ebony eyes flashing. She pressed the rest into her mouth, plunging a thumb up to a knuckle. She twisted her hand over, thumb still in mouth and eased it from between her full lips with a slow smack. Joelle knew what she was doing.

My throat tightened. I swallowed. "What," I squawked.

"These," she said, and raised a knee to tap my bag. "Gettin on their good side." She jerked her head in the direction of the guys as she snatched another donut hole.

Kyle sauntered by just then, humming *The Pink Panther* theme music. He and Joelle bumped hips as he grabbed a donut hole for himself.

"James, James. Can't you see?" he said, shaking his head. "You'll be fine."

I shrugged and looked down at my sneakers. And yet, despite Joelle's accusation of assholism, and the awkwardness of it all, my oliebollen plan seemed to be working. The sight of me walking into school between first and second hour evoked something of a Pavlovian response from the popular crowd. They'd smile, and there'd be high-fives all around.

Second hour Joelle and I sat next to each other in the third row of Mr. M's U.S. History class. Thin hair, dried red scalp, purplish nose, and transparent skin of a Scandinavian alcoholic. An analog clock the size of a manhole cover loomed on the wall above his desk. A gift from his family for completing his PhD, a degree he later admitted that he didn't quite finish.

"I'm only one paragraph away," he said one day, "from completing my doctoral thesis." His proud smile faded into a sentimental gaze at something beyond our heads, at something beyond everyone's reach. Especially his. It seemed a lot of teachers my freshman year were one paragraph away from something else. Something better, I was certain, than standing up in front of us.

Mr. M spent a lot of time talking about westward-pushing covered wagons. What time he did not dedicate to the daily struggle for survival out on the prairie—the deadly cold, scarlet fever, black wolves—he spent talking about himself. His exercise routine, his cooking, his physique.

"Under my clothes," he gushed, pink-faced and mostly to the girls, "my skin is practically wrinkle-free."

Mr. M traced a hand up his other arm, circling down to his belt buckle. He lifted his eyes from his waist a moment after I passed a note to Joelle.

Who's the asshole now?

She let out a snort. Mr. M unbuttoned a shirt cuff. Joelle held up her reply.

This is SO GROSS!!!

Mr. M continued about emollients, oils, salads, and skin care while pushing up a sleeve to reveal what he believed to be a wrinkle-free forearm. We rolled our eyes. Joelle and I couldn't even look at each other for fear of guffawing and getting detention, one of Mr. M's favorite threats.

In fact, at least once a day Mr. M's entire head flared varying shades of bright red and crimson as he ranted on and on that we ninth-graders simply didn't listen. "Not like in the old days," he'd say, and sigh wistfully as he handed out a detention slip. I don't know if the detentions ever made any of us a better listener, but the act of scribbling out one of those special yellow pieces of paper did seem to make Mr. M feel better for a little while.

Joelle and I passed the same note, the same sheet of spiral-bound notebook paper, back and forth all day long, each of us plucking and folding back the prongs of the frilly edges as we read each other's update.

I worked with Christina at my family's hardware store that night. Worked there nearly every night after school, in fact, except when I had CCD, a sort of "Sunday school" for Catholics run by the town's omnipresent nuns.

I liked Christina. She was a student at the local university and had a non-bossy big-sister way about her. Each night she unpacked her book bag and laid out class materials. She could usually find some time when not stocking shelves, pricing inventory, or clerking someone out to review notes for an important-sounding class like Classical Mechanics or Beyond Ethics. She was friendly and exciting and mellow and cool and smelled like the food co-op down the street. She was independent and looked like she actually managed to enjoy life and wasn't constantly miserable like me.

I told her about my mom saying that the University of Wisconsin was nothing but a party school, and that I should rule it out.

Christina wrinkled her nose. "*All* colleges are party schools," she said, the laughter coming over her in a wave.

After a while, she said, "Go to UW. Ya just gotta find a crowd that's not just there for a place to hang out while they drink beer for four years." She adjusted her glasses and tilted her head to a side. "And you will, James. I can tell. Trust me," she said, and smiled. Christina had a great smile. "You'll be fine."

The next day in Mr. M's class was more about black wolves and brutal survival conditions for settlers on those westward-pushing wagons. Joelle handed me a note as Mr. M turned his back to the classroom to erase something on the chalkboard.

Ask what people in Wisc. did with their dead during 1820s winters!!

I read the note twice and looked over at her. Holy shit. This was intense. Her black eyes shone. And just like that, Joelle became twice as beautiful to me.

The thought of the face Mr. M would make caused me to laugh aloud.

He spun and roared and drove a fist clutching the eraser into the slate behind him. His hand disappeared in an explosion of white dust.

"You don't fucking listen!" he shrieked. "None of you!" His red forehead flamed through light strands of combed-over hair.

We fell quiet, of course.

He turned to the chalkboard, breathing hard. Remained still for what felt like five minutes. Finally, he traced a finger along the crevice where he'd split the slate. He turned to us and placed a hand on a hip. A piece of green chalkboard fell to the floor and clattered.

He cleared his throat. A protruding vein on his forehead continued to throb like a purple worm. "I'm sorry I wasted your time with that," he said. He lowered his gaze and gestured behind him. He stooped to pick up the piece of slate. His blue slacks were smudged with white handprints. The manhole clock clicked.

No one moved.

"I'll fucking listen," Joelle called out, raising a hand. She pulled her black bangs aside and stared.

Somehow, despite being only marginally popular, the dark depth to her eyes that betrayed zero bullshit allowed Joelle to get away with this with Mr. M. He stepped over to his desk and sat down without a word. His chin twitched. He reached for a tissue and wiped his hands slowly. Then he pulled out another tissue and did it again. It was a spooky moment, as if Joelle willed him, toes dragging, across the classroom to his desk. The silence intensified like a liquid expanding behind the eyes. It was a silence I later connected to the vacuum created by a surge in Joelle's popularity.

The circle of guys I longed to crack—"The Inner Sanctum"—consisted of Bryant, Vince, Robert, Keith, and Kyle. Girls in the hot-chick clique called them Bry, Vinn, Robby, Key, and Ky. Which Joelle *loathed*. She mocked them mercilessly. "Ooh, Bryyy," she'd swoon, her voice going all high-pitched. She'd spin and flip her straight black hair around and let her knees buckle. She and I would sip sodas the way they did and laugh and laugh. Sometimes 7UP shot from our nostrils.

All these guys, except for Kyle, had parents who'd met in college. Their parents—an inner sanctum of another level—were put-together, had it going on. They were slim and active and hosted bridge clubs and cocktail parties and had big yards and helped out more than they should have on their children's school projects. They spoke with exultant voices and festive tones. They were volunteers and coaches and who knows what else. These people were everywhere, and their cars were always clean and smelled good inside. They were organized in a way that most kids' parents didn't have time for.

My parents' life resembled theirs more than it didn't, and they kept their relationships with this crowd—the parents of the popular kids—casual. Friendly, but not friends necessarily. Part of running a small-town Main Street business.

Kyle's family of eight lived crammed into a four-bedroom split with a brown and crunchy lawn. Tall grass gone to seed shot up along the stucco siding beneath a small picture window. Always exhausted, Kyle's probably once-attractive mom cussed a lot and mostly mailed motherhood in.

Kyle compensated with an attitude of moxie and bravado that gained him access to The Inner Sanctum. Yet you could see it gradually disintegrate, his inner *Pink Panther* wither, as we approached his house from up the block, and heard the sharp voices of his parents.

"I'm fuckin sicka raisin kids," his mom called out one day.

"Well, now what, Goddamn it?" his dad groaned.

"Oh, well, what do you *think*?" she snapped.

Kyle and I stayed out in the yard by the curb. He leaned against their old pickup truck that was always up on blocks. "Jesus Christ," his dad growled from somewhere inside the house. "Are you kiddin me?"

As kids, Kyle and I played trucks in the sandbox in my back yard and talked about being truck drivers for real when we grew up, all big and strong, toting freight from Boston to San Diego and eating at every Stuckey's along the way. Then we'd meet some girls in California and fly all the way back in a hot air balloon, circling Yosemite and Glacier National Park and trace the chain of Great Lakes to upstate New York.

We grew apart, though, as his physical maturity began to dwarf my twerpiness. But I don't think he ever forgot about our sandbox dreaming, or eating enough of my mom's cooking to become bored with it.

At lunchtime I pushed in at a table with The Inner Sanctum. I'd read Joelle's update, which usually covered a lot of ground. The number of bracelets that dipshit Kari was wearing. College recruiter visits she was happy to be still too young for. Her ogre parents.

The guys spoke of their weekend—either the one just past or the one to come—with relish. Always forbidden activities. The out-of-town high school football game. A jaunt up to the university arcade. Anything that involved getting into a car with teenage drivers.

Their chatter was all a bold underscore of my non-existent social life, all live and in color, in both the past and present tense.

"Don't worry," Kyle said, as I sat there glumly. "You'll be fine."

"Easy for you to say," I said. "You just do whatever the hell you want."

"Naw," he'd say, with sleepy eyes. "Trust me. You, James Kopek, will be fine."

Sometimes the way he said that made me wonder if he was saying the opposite about himself.

After lunch I had Mrs. B's Home Ec class while Joelle had Mr. N for Social Studies. Somehow, she'd slipped a note under the cover of my notepad. I pulled it out and read.

Are you going to the movie?

And there it was. The only legal thing that didn't require a car that kids my age could do in this town on the weekends was to go to the one-screen cinema across the street from my family's hardware store. Friday night was generally the night everyone my age went. "The movie" in this case was *The Deep*. After an entire summer and now a good part of fall of *Star Wars* showing daily at seven and nine o'clock—even the guys who'd made a lifestyle out of *Star Wars* lore were bored silly with seeing it so many times—a different movie had finally, mercifully, made its way to town. *The Deep*. Nine o'clock only. The seven o'clock showing would remain, until further notice, *Star Wars*.

It was a foregone conclusion in my mind that my parents would never let me go. Mom would have her reasons and then in private urge Dad to conjure something that needed doing down at the store.

I looked over for Joelle, seated three sets of cinder-block walls away in Social Studies, with yearning and confusion. She was practically asking me out. To a movie I couldn't comprehend her liking. How could Joelle, easily the brightest kid in the whole school, be drawn to a movie whose main selling point was a wet t-shirted Jacqueline Bisset? Joelle, the girl who with one effortless utterance managed to break a teacher simply by returning the volley of his very own words: *I'll fucking listen.*

The Deep, meanwhile, was a PG-rated movie that bent— and nearly snapped—the accepted norms of the PG movie rating, and therefore meant something more to us than just being a movie.

And then you had the nine-o'clock thing.

Nine o'clock was darkness. Nine o'clock was bedtime. Nine o'clock was adults-only R-rated films like *All The President's Men* and *The Godfather* and *The Exorcist*. *The Deep* at nine o'clock blew the lid off an untouchable Pandora's Box for us in a way that *Star Wars* at seven never could. And only the coolest among us would get to be a part of it. Which is probably why Joelle wanted to go.

I looked down at Joelle's note again. I'd completely forgotten where I was. Mrs. B . . . Home Economics. I felt hot. All I could see was Joelle seated in the theater next to some other guy with his hand on her slender thigh. Kyle, probably. Closest thing I had to a best friend at the time, which would serve me right. He was mostly Inner Sanctum. And now Joelle was, too. She'd be out of my league by year's end, I could tell. Dating upperclassmen and all that, while I cranked wrenches and drained oil from Briggs & Stratton engines at the store. I felt sick and avoided her the rest of the day.

I asked Mom after supper anyway. She was ready. She said no.

"But it's PG," I pleaded.

"Well," Mom said. "'PG' stands for 'Parental Guidance.' And as a parent, I am guiding you—"

I groaned and rolled my eyes. She folded her arms.

"That *actress* seems to think the only way people *like us* can be happy," she said, "is if she's showing off her..."

I knew it. Mom's fear was that I'd see a set of heaving breasts. My fear was that I never would.

I was likely not alone in my thinking. Ours was a town teeming with bitter CCD-teaching nuns—more numerous than trout—who admonished us, already guilty and condemned, with the occasion of our would-be sin, and the intricate connectivity of thoughts leading to other thoughts of increasing lasciviousness down an inevitably slipperier slope straight to Hell. Sister Vivian explained, happily aghast, about the "lubricated fire pole." About how something as innocuous as maple syrup dripping from one's chin could unwittingly result in one splashing down leagues-deep into eternal damnation. A shoreless lake of fiery excrement. Or worse, that you would cause someone else to land in Hell. Which of course would punch your one-way ticket to Hell, too.

In our town, sex was not a sin.

Sex was a miracle.

I looked at Mom and rolled my eyes and thought about how Bryant convinced his mom. Explained that seeing *The Deep* would be sort of like paging through one of his dad's girly magazines, except that on screen the girls were just moving around. And talking.

But Mom wasn't in a laughing mood. So instead, I explained what I understood to be the great story-telling aspects of *The Deep* based on what I'd gleaned from the back of the novel I'd seen lying around. It was a suspenseful thriller. Mystery and intrigue—Bermuda Triangle, after all. Scuba divers and shipwrecks. Geography lessons. A cultural endeavor. I should have stopped there but couldn't before mentioning the treasure hunters who discovered the bad guy's stockpile of morphine.

Mom pounced. "And drugs!"

Mom had already raised an entire family of teenagers through The Sixties and early Seventies, and was well-versed on the matter of drugs by the time I came along nearly a decade later. Drug stuff was old hat for her. A concern, yes. But old hat nonetheless. And Mom had *Prevention Magazine* on the nightstand and Paul Harvey at the far-right end of her A.M. radio dial to alert her of any new worries that had sprung up during my adolescence: The spiking dangers of sodium and cholesterol. The dubious morality of yoga. And the stimulating content of movies such as *The Deep*.

Mom shifted her weight to one hip and raised a coffee cup to her mouth, signaling an end to our conversation, and slamming shut the heavy stone lid on the sarcophagus of my social life.

I continued to buy donut holes for my friends as the rest of the week funneled toward *The Deep*. I felt like I was sinking into something deeper, too. Some certain kind of loneliness, an isolation I'd endure inside a hardware store helping John Deere loyalists like Mr. Colbian with carbed-up spark plugs or threading pipe for guys like Bob Ulrich. I checked the work schedule and saw that Christina would be working Friday night. So, there was that at least.

Joelle had become pretty enough during the past few days to fit in with the hot-chick clique. Her presence there seemed so natural now, as though she'd been an integral member of their clutch all along, and I'd never noticed. One day she showed up with curled hair parted down the middle, bangs feathered back on each side like Farrah Fawcett to reveal her instantly noticeable, instantly pretty face. It was like she became someone else overnight.

Meanwhile, what popularity I'd attained through donut holes had stagnated into irrelevance because by now it was well known that I was an uncool twerp, one lacking sufficient spine to defy his parents and partake in things like the dark depths of *The Deep*. And sensing my slipping grip on my social-standing in the middle of Mr. M's class, I blurted out Joelle's question concerning mid-winter corpse storage in Wisconsin.

Mr. M stepped away from the chalkboard. He looked at me gravely. I assumed another detention. Then his face went blank, and his forehead remained pale. He spoke as though a distant memory washed over him.

"Surviving family members stored their dead on the sloped rooftops of their homes..." Mr. M said. He drifted to his right and spoke in a way that made me wonder if some people around here still did this. "In order to keep cadavers safe from bears. The bodies then slid off the rooftops about the time it warmed up enough to dig." He paused for a thawing corpse to slip and thud in his memory. Or maybe it was his long-dead PhD. "And so, people buried their dead within a day or two of hitting the ground. 'Spring Digs,' they called it." He blinked and returned to the present. "Anything else?"

The class gasped. Mr. M walked over to his desk like a man sick or dizzy. "Anything else?" he repeated. I think he was looking at me, but it was hard to know. He rested a hand on his desk, taking measured breaths. Out of the corner of my eye I saw Joelle fold her arms. Mr. M tilted his head and I shook mine, stunned and doomed.

Friday arrived. Dad had me lined up to be at the hardware store after school getting things ready for some weekend sale he hadn't told me about. Dad's store was always neat, always ready, always prepared. The shelves were always stocked, and the merchandise always fronted. Always.

Back in the third row of Mr. M's class, Joelle handed me a new note on a fresh sheet of spiral-bound paper. *Are you going to the movie or not?* It landed more like a demand than a question.

I picked at the frilled edge and turned toward her with a somber face and downcast eyes. She pulled her bangs aside and looked away.

I fell into my store-closing routine at about 8:30 that night. This involved pulling the items on display from the front sidewalk back into the store. I was wrestling with a Ditch Witch when I heard loud talking swing around the corner from Johnny P's Pizza. I smelled cologne and perfume and looked up and saw Kyle along with the others.

"Kyle!" I yelped. I reached out and grabbed his arm.

He gave me a heavy shove and spun away. I guess I did yell his name pretty loud. His eyes narrowed and I saw him glance down at my hand. No oliebollen. The other guys looked beyond me and walked ahead, saying "C'mon, man" and "There's a long line!"

Across the street, a column of movie-goers talking excitedly trailed away from the main entrance of the theater and wrapped around the corner. I was dirty and sweaty, The Inner Sanctum standing on the sidewalk before me all showered, coiffed, and dressed for a night out. Kyle scoffed and stared, his mouth a frozen black gasp.

I glanced toward the store, where I was headed with the Ditch Witch, and saw Christina. She was reading. The curve of her hip rested against the checkout counter. Occasionally a hand raised absently to coil a strand of hair over an ear. And I finally saw her, really saw her. The way she held that book. Such ease and confidence. So comfortable in her own skin. Christina was a woman, I realized. One who could leave town whenever she wanted. Just leave. Leave and never come back.

Kyle, on the other hand, looked at me almost in a panic. He took a step away from the guys and toward me. I don't think the others could see it. But even if they could, their brains were already at the movie theater, already comfortable somewhere in their well-secured futures, all of them, each and every one, leaving Kyle far behind. Everyone, including me. *But you . . . you will be fine*, Kyle always said.

I stood on the sidewalk paralyzed and awash in his emotions. All negative ones. Kyle was entrenched in a past in which he would dwell for years and years. *Let me have this*, his eyes pleaded. *This is all I will ever have. This nowness.*

I felt so foolish. It was all right there in front of me, all this time. The looks from the rest of the guys, the hot chicks. They'd be gone in no time. For wherever their parents met in college.

And here was Kyle, at age fifteen, aware that he had already peaked. Or was just about to peak. And his glare, like the mask of moxie he wore to school, was all show for them, confession for me. He looked at me one last time, then looked away when he sensed this new understanding settle upon me.

Joelle emerged from behind the others. She came up beside Kyle and shot me a look with those onyx eyes that I didn't know what to do with. Could have been spite. Or maybe she was coming to Kyle's rescue. Didn't matter. She'd be gone, too. Some place like Cal Tech or Scripps. Then she raised and dipped a shoulder and turned Kyle around.

"Come on, Ky," she said, and linked arms with him. "You heard Bry. There's a long line already."

It was quiet inside the store.

Christina lowered her book and hooked a strand of brown hair over an ear. She pushed away from the counter and walked over to stand next to me. Together we watched the street.

"Friends of yours?"

I looked down at my boots. "Goin to the movie."

Christina smelled like a pita-pocket sandwich. I smelled like gasoline. I thought of Kyle's shirt where I grabbed him.

"Ah," she said. "*The Deep.*" She folded her arms and leaned back, sizing me up. "Eh, not to worry, James," she said.

I watched the street reflected in her glasses. The passing cars, a pedestrian wearing a bright green top. Christina's light-brown eyes moved from me to scan the front of the store, the copy of *Slaughterhouse-Five* she'd been reading between customers, and a receipt someone dropped on their way out. She squatted down to pick it up.

"Don't waste yer time," Christina said, standing up again. She shook her head and looked directly at me. "Saw it when it came out in Milwaukee. Seriously, James. It's . . . just some swimming tits." She slipped her book into a back pocket of her denim jeans. Her hair tossed gently. "*Star Wars* is way better."

Christina walked across the street to the movie theater after she zeroed out the cash registers. The line was gone and the street was dead. I pulled the remaining power equipment inside. She returned, triumphant, holding a large box of Junior Mints high over her head. We locked the doors and stepped into the cooling night of the empty streets. Black sky, low stars, the moon a white slit in the night above the cinema. She rattled the box at me. I looked at her, but my stomach was still all twisted up. I shook my head.

We walked. Christina said that some customers mentioned that bears had been spotted in the woods where the creek wove through campus. I told her what Mr. M said about keeping cadavers safe from bears when the ground was frozen.

She tipped candies into her mouth. Her jaw rippled and moved up and down. She slowed to a stop in front of the bakery. Through the window, the display trays that held the doughy dots of sweet oliebollen gleamed clean, shiny, and empty.

"Bullshit," Christina said, and swallowed. She was looking at me, but it was her reflection I saw doing the talking. "Come wintertime," she said, "bears hibernate."

Everyone Is Dead

Everyone is dead.

It's like a plot-twist for Sampo Andersen right as the story begins. All Sampo Andersen has to do is take his dog home from work. But when he and his somethingdoodle, Gleason, walk a few blocks from the 1950s Mid-Century Modern office building, Sampo Andersen finds himself very alone, staring down at a dead crow on the concrete sidewalk beside a colorful mosaic.

"Everyone is dead," he says to Gleason. Sampo Andersen smiles. Gleason looks around but does not respond. Sampo Andersen doesn't expect his dog to respond, but it would be nice if sometimes he did. Everyone is dead, he murmurs again in his head. "Including this crow," he says aloud. Gleason sniffs at the gleaming crow sprawled in the middle of the sidewalk. Sampo Andersen tugs his leash.

The crow calls to mind a game Sampo Andersen once played as a kid: Everyone Is Dead. It's a simple game of make-believe. If no one is around, and all is quiet, then it must logically follow that everyone is dead. The absence of everyone equals the existence of no one. Fun times, for a little boy, to go out on corpse patrol to seek out and recover elusive cadavers tucked away in city parks or beneath the floorboards of the Hauser's living room or stacked in neat cords at the Soylent Green plant down by the river. Any time no one was ever around equaled the game being suddenly afoot.

Sampo Andersen looks behind him past the basswood blossoms toward his office building, now out of sight beyond the humped street. He thinks of Yvette, the therapist in the office next door to his. She slipped a letter beneath Sampo Andersen's door, a letter which he nearly stepped on while walking out to use the restroom down the corridor.

Dear neighbor, the letter read. After months of sharing the same quiet office corridor, Yvette has yet to address Sampo Andersen by his given name. *This isn't a dog park or puppy playground. If you are unable to control your animal, you must leave it at home.*

Sampo Andersen stopped reading in the middle of the next paragraph, which rolled on to the next page. The letter continued for another page after that, all single spaced. He set the letter on his desk and left with Gleason.

Yvette doesn't seem like a very nice person for a therapist. But what Sampo Andersen knows of her, he only knows in passing. He attributes some of this non-niceness to her profession of re-assembling people back into being people again. He's seen the dark green pockets beneath Yvette's bleary eyes. He's heard her clients' sobs push through his walls. Hers is not easy work.

Sampo Andersen's work isn't exactly easy, either. Easy is how you describe other people's work.

No one really knows what it is exactly that Sampo Andersen does, but it's very demanding and very stressful. Remote mathy visualization involving data algorithms to predict fast-moving imaginary supply-chain management targets in an isolated environment, Sampo Andersen's place in the machinery of this industry figures as just one star in one constellation of one galaxy of separate yet united-by-the-magic-of-the-Internet co-collaborators. Meetings with distant colleagues take place mere feet in front of him through Sampo Andersen's high-resolution computer monitors. Reprimands and deadlines, too. Each co-worker blinks infinitely distant from their remarkable proximity, each their own star, each right in Sampo Andersen's face in on-demand convenience.

"You need thick skin for this job," his boss-in-another-time-zone sighs, wagging his head magnanimously through a pixel-perfect display. "You do, Samp. Ya just do."

Sampo Andersen's boss calls Sampo Andersen "Samp" for short. His boss's regular uttering of one needing thick skin for this hitting-of-fast-moving-imaginary-targets-and-getting-yelled-at-from-afar thing implies to Sampo Andersen that his boss feels that he himself is in possession of thick skin. Sampo Andersen disagrees. In Sampo Andersen's opinion, his boss does not have thick skin because in Sampo Andersen's opinion, his boss has no skin at all. Sampo Andersen's boss has scales.

A thin black line of ants advances in a spiral on the sidewalk behind Sampo Andersen and the dead crow at his feet and Gleason at his side. The thin black line swells, coils, and breathes in living ant art created courtesy of the woman who resides in the house in front of the sidewalk. Tight lawn edging frames each concrete sidewalk section into an individual canvas, which the woman, whose name Sampo Andersen can never remember—Rhonda?—hoses down and scrubs daily with a stout broom. As the day warms and the concrete dries, the woman draws shapes onto the cement squares by dispensing honey from squeeze bottles. Within the shapes of these lines, she applies syrup and molasses with broad brush strokes. The ants rise up from their small earthen mounds and come down from the trees with the rising sun and gleaming, heating slabs. The sticky honey stains the brown ants black.

The intricate outline of her honey opus, the woman's *opus ex mel*, jumps to life and quivers with pulsating throngs of ants. The syrup-and-molasses-filled outlines draw different colored species of ants, along with flying insects varying in coloration from bluish greens to burnt orange and muted fuchsias to create panels and spangles of contrasting hues: The leaves of a plant, the petals of a flower, the thorax of a bee, an impenetrable eyeball iris. Other images ranging from ornamental filigrees and sine waves to familiar renderings in the abstract like Kokopelli or today's Wheel of Dharma. All arranged daily by his neighbor and sort-of friend whose name Sampo Andersen can never remember. Joyce? The loops tighten and throb with ants. Gail? Sampo Andersen's dog pulls at the leash.

The battered crow lies fused to the concrete beside the Wheel of Dharma. An alien wheel. A large stenciled design made up of minute and hungry Earth ants, etched into the sidewalk like the vast Peruvian hillside desert carvings visible in their entirety only from high above the Earth's surface. The carvings that space aliens came down to Earth to help the Inca create. This occurred right around the same time they also helped the Egyptians and Maya build their pyramids and sphinxes and other massive structures. Then the space aliens left, their work here on Earth completed, never to come back except for that one time when they aided Michelangelo with some scaffolding ideas for his Sistine Chapel proposal. That took a while. This stenciling here resembles one of those alien-aided desert drawings, except that it fits within a sidewalk square and it is rendered with shimmering ants pulled involuntarily to honey and molasses.

The woman's yellow Minimal Traditional home is clutched in weathered cedar siding and peeling white trim. Inside, through a living room window framed by kelly green shutters, the walls of the dark interior throb a frosted twitching blue from the owner's high-definition television set. The owner sits on the front steps and flicks cigarette ashes into an empty beer bottle to her right, and drinks from a half-full brown beer bottle on her left. A pair of eyes the color of ice shavings flash at Sampo Andersen above small dark pockets, crescented symmetrically on each side of her nose.

Sampo Andersen sighs. The name of the not-nice therapist next door he can remember, this pleasant but odd woman's name he cannot. Her short brownish-blonde hair is wet and pressed into her scalp and drips onto her shoulders. A gray t-shirt and a pair of faded purple shorts hang loosely over her slack skin randomly tattooed green and blue. She smiles a tinged black. Her tongue is gray, the skin on her face flakes white from dryness and day-old makeup. One half of her face is lit up in bright sunlight, the other half stippled with small squares of leafy shade.

"Hello, Gleason!" the woman calls. The woman greets Sampo Andersen, too. She always remembers their names, and always calls Gleason's name first. Gleason is cuter. She smiles black and drinks wet beer and wipes her face with the back of a hand and wipes the hand on the fabric of her faded purple shorts. The fabric darkens and she inhales deeply from the end of a cigarette.

Sampo Andersen nods to her, tilts his head to the crow.

"Damnedest thing," the woman says, blowing smoke. Brenda? "Fell straight down outta the sky and hit right there, *thwap*. About twenny minutes ago." She sniffs and belches. "Barely missed my Dharma."

Sampo Andersen glances from the crow to the Wheel breathing with ant life. The Wheel throbs and churns like water flowing through a mill. The woman coughs and turns her head to look up and down the street.

Sampo Andersen breathes and looks up and down the street, too. Everyone is dead. Except for them. The woman shakes her head. "*Thwap*," she says again.

Sampo Andersen stares at the crow. Gleason strains at the leash and sniffs and pants. Sampo Andersen looks up for a place whence the crow may have fallen. There is none. The crow fell straight down from the middle of the wide blue sky. Sampo Andersen looks at the crow again. Gleaming black wings. Bent neck. Bulging dead eyes. The flies haven't noticed yet, but a blue jay has. A large jay has been cawing in alarm now, Sampo Andersen realizes, since he and Gleason rounded the corner by the burl oak at Don and Ron's a hundred feet away. It seems all Sampo Andersen can hear now is the hollering of that bird.

"We should call the DNR," Sampo Andersen says to the familiar but unnamed woman. His good friend Jared Kelmp has a masterful way of asking people for their name once forgotten. Almost makes it seem like a strength of character. Uses it to his advantage in a way that always eludes Sampo Andersen. He looks at the woman again.

"DNR used to wanna know bout dead crows," he says.

"The DNR?" the woman says, and draws in more air through her cigarette and sighs and swallows beer. "Do not resuscitate?"

Sampo Andersen looks at the dead crow and laughs.

"No," he says, and laughs again. "Department of Natural Resources. You know. Parks and rivers and lakes and such. Fish and deer and…" Sampo Andersen senses his mind wandering off. "Puma," he says with a smile. "And they may wanna know . . . about this crow."

"Huh," the woman says, and flicks ashes at the bottle. "No shit."

"Ja," Sampo Andersen says. "West Nile virus."

"West Nile?" She pulls at her cigarette again. "This part of the state? Yer sure?"

"Yup. The virus has been encroaching on the upper Midwest. They used to ask people to report dead crows. Cuz they die right away."

"Huh." She shakes her head slowly. "Canary in a coal mine," the woman murmurs. "Well," she says, leaning back on her hands and straightening her torso. "I can't call cuz I gotta leave for the airport."

"Oh."

"Ja. Pickin up my ma. Flyin in tuh-day," she says.

Gleason strains at the leash for the dead crow. The dog whines. This whining makes Sampo Andersen think of the not-nice therapist next door at work, who explained how Gleason disrupts her trauma patients' trauma therapy sessions. Their expensively schooled PTSD service dogs in particular. And a trauma patient cannot be having a PTSD dog required to listen to frequent barking from the poorly trained canine rabble next door.

Sampo Andersen is pretty sure he suffers from PTSD, too. Gleason is a comfort. Not a bona-fide PTSD service dog, but one who extends simple canine comfort to a frequently distraught human nonetheless. The therapist next door knows nothing of Sampo Andersen's past. The powerful moments he recalls paralyze. The cruelty of wealthy adolescent jocks. The terror, humiliation, and outright physical pain of their locker-room torture tactics. And the joy of goading and cackling coaches.

A pair of cheerful Mormon missionaries canvasses homes on the next block. One raises his arms, shirt sleeves as white as a newborn cloud, to greet a face that's appeared from behind a just-opened door. Someone else who isn't dead. The Mormons aren't dead, either. They may never die. Sampo Andersen wonders what you call a group of Mormons. Gaggle of geese, pod of dolphins, skulk of foxes. He looks from the crow to the white-shirted Mormons again. A smile creases Sampo Andersen's right eye.

Sampo Andersen looks up at the woman with the dry skin and loose flesh and beer-bottle ashtray who's gotta go to the airport. The makeup packed into the grooved squint lines around her eyes reveals more than it conceals.

"Fine," Sampo Andersen says, "I'll call."

"The DNR," the woman says. She lifts her chin. Her nose brightens within a square of sunlight. She raises her cigarette hand.

"Ja," Sampo Andersen says. "The DNR. Sorta."

Sampo Andersen dials the non-emergency phone number for the local police department. A receptionist listens to Sampo Andersen and transfers him to County Dispatch. County Dispatch is an emergency number. "This isn't an emergency," Sampo Andersen starts to say, sensing it's too late. "I just—"

"Nine-one-*one*," Dispatch insists. "What is the nature of your emergency?"

Sampo Andersen sighs. "No emergency," he says, and looks up from the crow at the woman still seated on her steps. This woman whose name he can never remember, this woman who now allows him to forgive Yvette, the not-nice therapist in the office next door at work, for never bothering to learn or remember his. This woman with the skin that peels from her face in flakey square makeup chunks.

The flakey-makeup-lifting-and-peeling-from-her-cheeks-in-square-chunks-and-taking-flight thing is pretty weird. But nothing new.

"Justa dead crow," Sampo Andersen says. "Does the DNR still wanna know about these?"

"A dead crow," Dispatch asks.

"Ja. I was just tryin to get through to a DNR agent, so I called the non-emergency phone number here in town, and they routed me to you."

The woman with the beer bottle ashtray stands up and grunts and stretches her back and turns into her house. A trail of makeup flakes and cigarette ashes swirls within a current of air pushed from the door closing behind her. The bluish frosted glow inside drops from the walls. She's snapped off her enormous television set. The ant coils behind Sampo Andersen swell and sprawl in Sampo Andersen's direction. It's only a matter of time, Sampo Andersen thinks, until the ants abandon the sidewalk squirts for this crow's dead eyes.

Sampo Andersen and Dispatch are silent. Sampo Andersen can hear chatter in the background at County Dispatch. The chatter of non-non-emergency business: Burning buildings, exploding hearts, missing children, beaten wives, drowning drunks. Sampo Andersen shakes his head. He has a dead feathered reptile at his feet next to curvy spirally sidewalk ant art.

A different woman, one who resembles Yvette, staggers into view from behind the burl oak at Don and Ron's place. She wears a Jell-O green jacket. Lengths of thin hair wander above her scalp within an electric breeze all its own. She appears to be breathing hard, but she is just far enough away that it's hard to tell for sure. Maybe it is Yvette. And that is simply how Yvette breathes when walking around out in the wild, away from the office building. But what would she be doing out here, anyway? Yvette doesn't live anywhere near here. Her steps are labored, uncertain, and deliberate. But there's more, and Sampo Andersen can sense something is very wrong.

"I..." he says, and turns for his neighbor, and a name to call her by. But the woman is behind a closed screen door inside her house. Sampo Andersen can't remember her name anyway. He only remembers Yvette's name because it's written on a name plate beside her door which he walks by several times a day.

"I'll connect you," Dispatch says, after what seems like five minutes but in truth is less than one second. "I'll connect you to a DNR agent's voicemail. Please leave a useful message—"

"Wait!" Sampo Andersen yelps. Yvette, closer now, is not Yvette. She's an Yvette-a-like who looks right through Sampo Andersen with kaleidoscopey Mayan mural eyes. She takes another terrible stride. A stream of blood surges from her nose and her eyes curl white straight back into her head.

"Puppy," she gasps, her voice an echoing whistle as though a hole has been pierced through her neck at the back of her mouth. "Puppy," she breathes again. Air squeezed through a ready kettle's spout. Her stride convulses and her legs accordion beneath her and twist like a bent drill bit. She hits the sidewalk. Sampo Andersen and Gleason yelp and jump back.

"Look, this is really weird," Sampo Andersen blurts, his stomach curdled from the sound of the Yvette-a-like's face splatting on cement. "But while calling you about a dead crow on this sidewalk, I—"

"You're calling about a dead crow, correct?"

"Yes. But while—" Another attempt from Gleason to lunge at the bird.

"I can pass along your information to a DNR agent."

"OK. Thanks. But while calling you, this woman—"

"Name and phone number please."

"But…" Sampo Andersen hesitates, but then quickly complies with Dispatch. The only movement from the Yvette-a-like has been the ooze of blood from her nose into a dark puddle.

"I . . . Ma'am!" he shouts to the woman on the sidewalk.

Sampo Andersen ventures a tentative step towards Yvette. The woman who isn't, but who looks like Yvette. The treetops tilt and twist above. A sharp snapping sound that Sampo Andersen recognizes makes him stagger. It is the sound of the spinning Earth picking up and skipping from its axis. The flakey makeup lady whose name Sampo Andersen can never remember steps from her house. The screen door slaps hard against the threshold. She scratches at a cheek, releasing another light plume of particulate DNA, and looks at Sampo Andersen looking at the bleeding woman sprawled face down on the concrete two sidewalk sections away from the woman's sidewalk ant art. She sniffs and wipes her mouth and tells Sampo Andersen she's gotta go to the airport.

Sampo Andersen turns and blinks and nods. His breath is cold. Gleason pulls in three separate directions, almost all at once: The Yvette-a-like, the flakey makeup woman, the dead crow. Sampo Andersen explains the situation to Dispatch. Dispatch is unfazed by the nature of one emergency occurring during the reporting of another. Yvette-a-like is breathing but she doesn't move, her frail hair clumped with sidewalk blood. The woman with the flakey makeup skin pulls away in her mid-1970's Monte Carlo. She's gotta go to the airport. A siren's shriek filters through neighborhood tree limbs. The incessant blue jay flees. Pulsating sidewalk ant art coils sprawl and widen like frayed rope.

"I'll now connect you," Dispatch says, "to a DNR agent's voicemail box. Please leave a meaningful message, being sure to include your name and a reliable phone number you can be reached at. Thank you."

Her voice cuts out. A ringtone growls in Sampo Andersen's ear. An agent's voicemail greeting greets Sampo Andersen several growls later. He leaves a meaningful message, his name, and a reliable phone number he can be reached at.

EMTs arrive, revive, collect, and depart in the span of a single sentence. ER bound. Sharp sirens wail and Doppler away into diminished sighs. Sampo Andersen glances back at the dead crow, still splayed, head still cocked in an angle of disbelief, iridescent black feathers a glinting purplish bruise in the late sun. He and Gleason continue their walk. They step around more coils of quickening ants. Sampo Andersen guesses this piece of sidewalk ant art spans five or six yards. The neighborhood is quiet and empty again. Everyone is dead.

Almost.

Sampo Andersen sees a figure moving about in the next house. A person. A not-dead human person. He and Gleason slow their stride. Maybe it was just the curtains. Rustling on the other side of the mossy grass of the person's yard. A heady light-headedness comes over Sampo Andersen at the thought of another person seeing what just happened here and not helping. He feels the same chill he feels when he talks to his boss. And he wonders about his boss, the reptilian-skinned man. What it's like to slither home, to shed that skin. Pull out of that old husk. Then, all of a sudden, those fresh new scales all slick and glistening. The utter relief of release. Sampo Andersen straightens. Certain women in Sampo Andersen's friendship circle speak of pedicures in like tones. He wonders if Yvette, or the not-Yvette Yvette-alike, or even the alien-ant-art woman for that matter, ever gets her toes done.

The EMTs are long gone. Who was that woman? It wasn't Yvette, though it certainly looked like her. She's reached that magical invisible middle-age at which everyone who isn't dead becomes transparent and looks nearly exactly alike.

Sampo Andersen takes a breath, and nods. He will continue his walk, take his dog home, and that will be that. Gleason will reach adulthood. Gleason will woof less. And it will be good. Sampo Andersen looks at the house in which he saw movement. Not a person. Just the curtain moving in the breeze. So all is good and everyone is dead again.

Almost.

Sampo Andersen's phone rings. He turns from the non-person-curtain yard-moss to the sidewalk. The ants glisten and the sun slides across the thick blue sky. His phone rings again. Sampo Andersen breathes. His heady light-headedness begins to pass. The number on the phone's clean display seems familiar enough, so Sampo Andersen answers. The caller identifies himself as a State of Wisconsin DNR agent. Sampo Andersen explains about the dead crow up the sidewalk from Don and Ron's.

"Oh," the agent says. "Ja," he says. He sounds disjointed. Sampo Andersen senses the DNR agent pat body parts for a pen. "Just throw it away, then."

"What?" Sampo Andersen scoffs. "I thought you wanted to know—"

"West Nile has been here a few years now. And so," he sighs, "we're no longer recordin dead crows."

"Oh."

"Ja. Prolly just died from some 'rodent control' program?" Sampo Andersen can hear the air quotes. "Got inta some poison by eatin something that got poisoned. Carrion or whatnot. Sad, really. Looks like an easy meal . . . ends up bein deadly, though. So just sweep the thing up inta a Target bag or whatever and jus throw it away, then."

"Uh. Okay. I'll tell the owner when I see her."

Sampo Andersen senses the DNR agent shrug.

"The owner of the place the bird was found in frunna," he says. "Thing died smack in the middle of the sidewalk." Sampo Andersen glances around. "She had to go to the…"

Sampo Andersen's eyelids become heavy and pull shut in one . . . two . . . three tugs. The trees rattle and release a strong breeze. Near an alley entrance, a plastic Target bag crackles and tumbles into view. His brain slides along, in and out of the Target bag that he wants to tell the DNR agent won't work because it won't fit over the dead crow because the crow is a crazy-smart-beautiful-winged-flying thing. Even dead, it, too, is a magnificent and breathtaking work of art.

The tilt of the sidewalk ant artist's neck and dripping hair fade into view. Her shaved-ice eyes stare straight ahead, lost in thought, motoring down that highway. The dry skin on her face flaking and pulled out the driver's-side window of that Monte Carlo. Sylvia? He's completely out of guesses now. A decidedly introverted thinker, this woman.

Sampo Andersen stares at the sidewalk, the honey Dharma. Smells like summer cement and hot ants. Sampo Andersen doesn't know what hot ants really smell like, but he knows what he thinks of when he thinks of the smell of hot ants. He sniffs again and stares at the charcoal crow and wonders if the manufacturers of Soylent Green ever made a Soylent Black. Everyone is dead.

Sampo Andersen hears the DNR agent speak. His toes want to reach out through his shoes to touch the moss. He wants to tell his slithering boss with his fresh new scales about the moss, too. About what he's missing. The DNR agent says something else.

Sampo Andersen looks at the crow, the empty sidewalk, the cobalt sky, Gleason. And his plot, twisted from the very beginning of all of this, a bend in the arc of his life's through-line careening here between the dead crow, the collapsed Yvette-a-like, and the gleaming Wheel of Dharma, pulsating with infinite continuous cycles of life.

There is a satisfying click as his planet reattaches to its axis and begins to spin once again. Sampo Andersen looks up the sidewalk, down past the burl oak at Don and Ron's on the corner, and back. The murder of Mormons bisects a cross-street one block away and disappears from view around a house. Gleason whimpers. The Mormons are gone. All is good, and everyone is again dead.

Sampo Andersen squats beside the alien ant art. After a moment, he drags a fingertip through a cord of ants. Gleason whimpers. Sampo Andersen sticks the fingertip into his mouth. He smiles. Gleason tugs. The honey tastes like ants.

Goat Milk

First you hear it. Then you smell it. And finally you see it. Spray paint. A hulking crew donning luminous haz-mat gear inscribes the tell-tale letters BSW across the front of the yellow house opposite yours.

Black Scap Waxing. Street name for the fatal virus currently traversing the North American continent. A dark rash resembling the shape of a waxing moon spreads in torturous fashion to fill the lunar cavity of the victim's scapula. It starts as a burning itch and quickly moves into an unrelenting agony as the waxing heightens. The scabbing rash suppurates into a slimy film, which hardens to form a gleaming, crusted crown. The patient becomes unable to sit upright except to wail or shriek.

There is no treatment, no vaccine, no cure. Death generally arrives within ten days if the BSW Haz-Matters thumping up your walk do not.

You thought you heard a remote wail during the night, and it occurred to you that this virus should be called Black Scap Wailing. And you're pretty sure your wife has it. Though she's not yet waxed, not yet loosed an agonized cry.

Cries heard from windows result in prompt calls to BSW Dispatch. A truck quickly arrives. Haz-Matters attach a white corrugated corridor to the front door leading out to the truck. They vacuum up the families inside and drive away. You don't know where they never come back from. But you've heard things. Cremation. Ashes of humans shoveled into a communal urn. Flushing.

All possessions, all items connected to the virus in any way, must be incinerated: Clothes, carpets, furniture, books, homes . . . bodies.

Morning has barely broken, but it's already hot. Your phone vibrates. *Barneses got BSWed*, a text from the neighbor across the street reads. Spattered paint gleams painfully bright. Like blood from a fresh brand on the rump of a steer.

Yeah, I saw, you type, on full display before your picture window. You close your robe. Spray-paint stench filters in.

Still need that milk? she asks. You look across the street to her porch and tap on your phone to strike a quick deal. You get a move on.

Upstairs, you peek beneath the sheet covering your sleeping wife. You need to check before going outside. Just so you know. She doesn't move. Her slender back is clean, creamy, and beautiful. Not waxing. But she smells sick. Not rotting-flesh sick, just feverish split-lip sick. You exhale and lower the sheet.

Outside is not for everyone. There's the lockdown, for one. And danger for another—the air is poison, the people violent.

You strap on a surgical mask to go out anyway. The BSW truck gasps and pulls away with the Barneses bundled and pushed inside. You nod a farewell. They can't see you. Probably can't see anything.

You peer out your front window at your neighbor again. The risk of crossing the street is enormous, even for bartering. Every home a cruise ship, violations are punishable by law—a forty-day remote quarantine plus $50,000 fine—since the virus mutated and went airborne in February. Now you need a government-issued letter to validate departures for your job if you still have a job and if the government agrees that your job is essential. Plumbers, electricians, liquor store clerks, prostitutes.

You still have a job, too. The economy is brittle, and you throw the entirety of your self at it to prove your worth and not get canned. There's no time to look for something better and they know it.

You drag a bale of home-spun toilet paper outside. Taught yourself to render newsprint into toilet paper last time around. You liquefy and soak pulp and the ink separates into a foam you scrape away and then out come squares of recycled paper.

Toilet paper became *the* joke and *the* symbol of the last pandemic. Panic purchases and hoarding resulted in overwhelmed and incapacitated supply chains. This time, the supply-chain problem has gotten ahead of the supply chain itself: There are regular shortages of everything from beer to bacon to insulin to shoelaces because there is no gasoline for transport because the oil companies ceased production when the price of oil crashed when people stopped driving because of the global lock-downs.

You need to calculate a tree-to-tree path for acquiring the goat milk, something you desperately need. Thankfully the trees in your neighborhood are hundreds of years old. Broad trunks provide ample cover.

A burgeoning itch takes root beneath an eye. Tickles like a tick. You want to scratch it, but know not to. Bad enough you're outside in the first place. It's like when your job as a hospital orderly was to transport an AIDS patient—Colin?—to chemotherapy. Once scrubbed and garbed, you could not touch your face. Rock Hudson was newly declared positive, and NASA's fleet of Space Shuttles was all still intact. Yeah, Colin sounds right. Just soap, scalding-hot water, stiff nail brushes, head-to-toe latex, goggles, and masks. And a stout head nurse to hover over your sterile field.

The neighbor on her porch has been ready for this for nearly twenty years. Taught herself how to raise chickens and grow herbs and vegetables and graze goats in her back yard. She also learned how to churn butter meanwhile she patiently armed herself to the teeth. Nuclear war, economic collapse, famine, epidemic. She wasn't sure. *The Birds*, maybe. She just woke up one day with the revelation that she'd better learn how to churn her own butter pretty damn fast.

But she knew. Knew that whatever was coming, was coming for us all. And she's been smug ever since. Yet, even she needs things. And she knows that you've managed to recycle newsprint into toilet paper. Somehow. It's all nebulous magic to her, but she doesn't care. She's willing to trade a gallon of her goat milk for a bale of your butt wipe. Seems fair.

The suggestion of one wood tick crawling on your skin launches an entire flotilla of imaginary ticks scuttling across your body, clawing into every sticky crevice.

The sun continues to rise, the air no longer a golden post-dawn fairyland, and you are taking far too long to get to your neighbor's house. You send a text. *Almost there.*

The trunk of another fat oak is rough and hot against your back as you eye her reply: *Leave it on the steps and hurry the f- up.*

A BSW truck passes, crew all haz-matted up inside. You ease from behind the oak. Probably didn't see you. Texting and driving. Worry for your wife consumes you. The two of you haven't been getting along so well the past several months. But everyone is tense these days, and your current need for goat milk trumps all that.

You only broke your sterile field once. Touched your face before entering a stark white room in which sat a solitary Colin. You had to disrobe, re-scrub, and re-garment while Colin shivered away, waiting and dying.

You look up and see your neighbor on her porch. You don't want to break her sterile field, either. It's as if a transparent veil hangs draped from her eaves like a gelatinous force field that jiggles and triggers alarms when touched.

Maybe it's just a bug your wife is coming down with. You'll check her temperature again when you get back, assuming she's not already shrieking.

You place the bale on your neighbor's step. She's left the goat milk near the sidewalk. Down the street, the BSW truck bends around a corner. You make a subtle show of placing a boot on the sturdy bale to make it clear to people peeping from behind every window pane that all you're doing is bartering, hoping they'll let you slide.

God, your eye.

Your neighbor says something and you look up, knowing you should leave. Get home. She grumbles about government leaders and their blame games. Why won't she let you leave? Lingering is risky. Then it's obvious she suspects something about you, that she's holding you up intentionally. And now you're in the position of her reporting you if you leave prematurely, yet getting caught if you stay too long. She smiles. You're hiding something. She has one of those new SaniChat® masks. Designed to facilitate dialogue, its transparent shield allows you to see the speaker's mouth. But there's no need for lip-reading now. It's clear what's up.

She asks about your wife. You shrug.

"Been a while…" she says. Her eyes flick towards your house. You explain that to reduce exposure and risk, it's just been you running all the errands. She nods and looks away, unconvinced.

A screen door bangs nearby. Rory, one house over. Leaving for his beer-and-bait shop. You traded him for squirrel meat in the dark the other night. So did your neighbor.

The two of you fall silent. Birds sing. More coffee would be good. Taking your wife's temperature and scratching your eye would be good, too. A recollection of what Rock Hudson's death did for AIDS awareness comes to mind. And how in your house the real tragedy was the shock of his homosexuality, not what disease would soon mean.

She nods and you nod. The sweating quart bottles of goat milk clank when you hoist the galvanized tote. You return the way you came.

"An older man…" your mother-in-law said, a decade ago, when your wife told her about your first date. She folded her arms and looked at her daughter knowingly. "Well," she said. "They only want one thing, ya know…" She jutted her chin and looked away.

"He can have it," your wife said.

You smirk and chuckle, home only a half-block away. Then, in the blackest part of your brain, a rash waxes between your wife's shoulder blades, and someone has already called BSW Dispatch. Your eye begins to water. Profusely. Colin had watery eyes. Lost pounds by the day, grew noticeably lighter with each lift.

You're relatively certain that your wife won't wail. Not with the windows open.

You wonder about the last time you rode in an elevator, waited in line, went anywhere, what day it is. Or thought about Colin.

Your eye twitches. "Hold me," Colin whispered, shrinking in your arms, his bony elbows hanging around your neck. "Just hold me," he murmured, and pressed his cold fingers into your back. "Please…"

You look at the red BSW insignia on the Barnes home, twitching eye quivering shut. A tinge of spray paint lingers.

A wail from your open bedroom window splinters the quiet morning air. At your feet lies the curved walkway to your front steps, its winding route always conjuring fond memories of your childhood, walking along coiled pathways and routes through lush yards and gardens, arms held out straight like a tightrope walker.

Another visceral wail, and your eyes follow the pavers to where your adult path leads.

Maybe you scratched at your eye just now, mere steps from your porch. Your wife's shriek, your gasp, the turn of your head, the reach to scratch, those scuttling ticks. You don't know.

But you do know that you kept your field sterile for Colin that day, though you wouldn't hold him like he asked. You were too scared. And he shivered alone in a white, white room. Watched you walk away.

You place the glass bottles of goat milk into the fridge and leave a note about your baby. Your wife stopped lactating after only five weeks, and your baby will be hungry when they come.

You curl into bed with your wife, touch her hair and let her bury her nails into your palms and draw blood, again and again. Your hands grow red and wet. Haz-Matters thump up the stairs.

Unresolved

It begins with a certain image, say that of a young woman who performs a ring-scan of a waiter's left hand as he removes a beer glass from an outdoor table at a sunny, leafy café (and, let us make no mistake, the enticement offered here is nearly immediate:

Who is she?

What does she look like?

Why is she there?

Is she waiting for someone? If so, who?

Is she reading something? If so, what?

iPhone or Android? We can assume, given her age and the current year, that she owns such a device. Yet for now, we can't speculate which because at the moment she happens to be one of the few patrons at the café not looking at hers while seated outside at that table beneath all those leaves on this spectacular September afternoon.

Ah, she's reading. Good. A book. Hardcover. But…

Is she there to read so as to pass the time while waiting for a certain person? Does she intend to study? Wait. Now she reaches for a menu. Aha. She is preparing to place a food order! But what will happen when the food arrives? Will she actually eat it? Or will she allow it to rest on her table until it stagnates or congeals in the open air, like a thick potato soup gone to chill, then declare herself no longer hungry?

Hard to know until the narrative gives more. Such as:

Philippa Peters chooses a shady, outdoor table at The Ledge Like White Elephants Café & Patisserie overlooking the icy and appropriately named Noisy Creek. A dark recess to match her dark mood, despite this bright, glorious late-summer's day. It's days like this, she sighs, that explain why people actually choose to live in this part of the country. She leafs through a book, finds the spot where she left off reading earlier this morning while using the Ladies room, and resumes, now more content in her dark mood seated in her dark shady spot at a coveted outdoor table at a café most locals refer to as *The Ledge*, though some, like Pip, just call *Elephants*.

A very tall, long-legged waiter stands over her. She turns her head to his voice to find herself directly confronted with his crotch. Or, rather, the button-fly of the khakis providing stylish, yet comfortable cover for said nether region. Pip raises her chin to look up at him. He tilts his head to a side to speak. The sun is directly behind him and all she can see is a dark silhouette of a man wearing glasses.

Pip's food arrives promptly. Butternut squash soup, served with several slices of this morning's batch of dark rye bread, freshly sliced, and a small cheese plate. Pip is an eater. She tears at the bread and breaks off a piece of cheese and looks down at her book. The world disappears.

Pip has requested a glass of local beer, which has not arrived. A black beer. The soft bread catches in her throat and she looks up. Her tall waiter is nowhere in sight. She looks back at her book, and the world disappears again.

Beneath the canopy of oaks, elms, and willows just over the steep limestone ledge beyond Pip, a crouching fisherman has performed magic—the real thing—and pulled a gleaming trout from the frigid underworld of a quiet pool of the dark stream forty feet below. Noisy Creek. So clear and cold it will crack your teeth. Moments later, the trout flips in red, wet, golden flashes upon broad emerald lichen stones beneath the man's outstretched hand.

Two tables away a young man and woman sit opposite one another. The two are silent, their drinks unmoved and untouched. Their arms extend across the small outdoor table toward each other, holding smart-phones. They gaze at their phones, which once, twice, then again a third time, nearly touch. The two do not speak, their eyes do not meet.

Pip is grumpy, and needs to eat. She's discovered a typo in the book she is reading. At least, she feels it's a typo. A typo, or a very cruel ruse played by the author, who began a parenthetical statement on page seventeen with a left parenthesis, (, and now, two hundred thirty-seven pages later, has yet to close it with a matching right,), thereby rendering virtually the entire book a mere aside to whatever it is that the author will eventually get back to, and she reads the full two hundred thirty-seven pages in a corresponding state of intake of breath, as one does in anticipation of whatever it is being added to the writing of whatever has been written and remains to be completed. It's the sort of intake of breath that accompanies the anticipation at the very beginning of a ring scan of a person of interest. And now, as she flips the page, the brunt of the book continues to remain in a state of unresolved discomfort and discord. And still ringless. Seems to match her life of near misses and lackluster achievement back in her small dead-end town, a life up to this point wadded up and trapped, by its incompleteness perhaps, within an open-ended parenthetical statement.

Years after high school, Pip read in a psychology journal that high school is for finding one's sense of self. This comes in handy once one reaches college, which, according to the article, is generally regarded as a time an individual finds a sense of vocation or career. This was news to Pip, currently occupying that nebulous space between semesters off from college while still living in a college town. College, her father had told her, really only teaches one how to learn. About all Pip learned while going to college was that she didn't care much for going to college. Mostly, her issue had to do with lighting. Too bright or never light enough and always of poor quality. Classrooms, study areas, dining rooms, libraries, restrooms, gymnasiums. All too industrial, all too metallic, all of it.

This issue with poor, or excessive, mechanical lighting was that it affected her sleep and thus stifled her ability to wake up in the morning and called in to question the need to arise at 6:45 for agonizing Theory of Gravity labs. Why? she'd asked. Just to prove, for the ninety-ninth consecutive time that a bag filled with sand nudged from a table's edge will fall to (or, per her professor, 'collide with') the floor? Day after day, Pip documented and charted the phenomenon of sand-bag-and-floor collisions with precise detail. Pip earned a grade of ninety-nine percent for this particular lab exercise, an exercise that Pip now tells friends functioned as a covert test for the existence of personality, as if her physics lab had been hijacked by a psychology prof conducting research. The one hundredth bag she threw out the window. *Object No. 100: Failed to succumb to irresistible force*, she noted, with considerable satisfaction. *For once.* The object failed, but Pip did not. She succeeded in earning a very expensive F. Which is why today she chose this shady space in which to track down that missing right parenthesis the nasty little toad of an author has yet to get around to plunking down in what she now suspects to be yet another clandestine test. She glances around the patio. Filtered sunlight all around. Lots of natural light here, and a healthy amount of natural darkness, too.

She wonders about her friend, Elspaith. She'd wanted to hang out with her today, just be near her smell. But Elspaith had to work. Again. Elspaith runs her mother's bakery in Noisy Creek and is always working. Middle of the night, early morning, late morning, early evening. Always. She works like they do in the dead-end town Pip came from. Elspaith probably made the bread Pip's been eating and is probably right now doling out loaves and rolls and pastries and goofy grins in stride to any and all who enter. Pip chews. She thinks Elspaith is beautiful, and this one, on her tongue, feels like an Elspaith bread.

The waiter's crotch returns bearing Pip's black beer. She nods, making a conscious effort not to do so directly at that nearby point where his legs join, and takes a deep drink. The black beer is cold. Perfect day for this. Warm, mid-September afternoon with a musky autumn essence woven crisply into the fabric of the air. The cool, damp breath rising from the creek below soon will form creeping mist tendrils, an inching mist that glides across the patio in a slow sprawl, encircling the tables and chairs, enveloping diners one and all. This excites Pip. She scrunches up her bare shoulders as a chill trickles up her spine.

The soup, bread, cheese, and beer improve Pip's mood. There are few things that cannot be solved with cheese, her mother once said. And mustard. Pip's mother, who also grew up in the same dead-end town as Pip, made all her own mustards, eleven varieties that Pip was aware of.

Pip considers her mother. Pip, like her mother, is a product of yet another of the same incessant thread of families regenerated, one after another, generation after generation of one continuous, virtually identical closed loop of laps run or cycles spun in their compact community on the Wisconsin side of the Upper Peninsula of Michigan. Haylow. The same faces, hair, eyes, ears, brains, laughs, and sneezes. All the same family batch one after another, right down to the farts. Occasionally an artist, scientist, or a talented athlete. But mostly almost always just the same versions of themselves, with the intermittent relief of a new family tree—say, a new physician to replace the one who died—to take up residence with her family and provide some new faces for the local kids to play with and possibly more before they tired of Haylow and moved on. Always temporary, new-comers soon became soon-leavers. But for the most part the Cernohouses are happy to once again have their children grow to become best friends with the Scammells, for example, who feel mutually toward the Cernohouses, both of whom hold great animosity for the Harlens and Jurkins clans, who hate everyone but themselves and each other. Such is the daily drama of provincial American life out in The Middle.

The small-town, dead-end clans are, in part, what has landed Pip here at the café in far-flung Noisy Creek, Wisconsin. She had to get out of Haylow if for no other reason than to disrupt the monotony of surnames and snow-scorched, pasty faces. Break the spell. She was born a Peters from Haylow. The Peterses have always been close friends with those Cernohouses and Scammells. They golfed, fished, hunted, knitted, cooked, prayed, ate, worshipped, gossiped, and sat in book clubs together, and frequently expected to pair up and inter-marry. Except for this bunch. Pip detests the modern-day incarnations of Cernohous and Scammell offspring, much to the dismay of all Peters, Cernohous, and Scammell parents and elders, worsened by Pip's departure for Noisy Creek, the town's name uttered in contemptuous snorts and sneers by her contemporaries Jaleb Cernohous and Sherri Scammell as "One of them *university* towns."

Pip continues to eat. She doesn't mind her dark moods, really, though she worries about things that her mother worries about. Her mother worries that Pip's not worried about things that a woman her age should be worried about, and right now Pip finds that sort of worry, worrying in a fashion of her mother about what her mother worries about, to be most worrisome for a young woman such as herself.

Pip realizes that she's drank nearly all of her beer when the waiter's crotch reappears at her side. Her eyes move to the nearby couple, phones now more intimate, then to the hand wrapped around her beer glass and connected, eventually, to the crotch clutched in khakis, to scan for a ring. Pip doesn't really care if there is a ring, she's merely curious. She stares at the bright orange leaves of a nearby maple, which has turned about a month early.

She stares at the flaming orange leaves for so long that when she looks back up she sees only the pulsating outlines of bright orange leaves against the waiter's dark silhouette. Pip tells the orange pulsations that fade back into a face again connected to the body of the waiter's crotch she would like another beer please. He removes her empty soup bowl, leaves the remaining cheese and slice of black bread, nods, and crosses the patio in four strides. The rear door opens and she hears hollering from the kitchen. Normal kitchen hollers.

Nothing to be worried about. She will tell her mother up in Haylow that there's nothing to be worried about.

Pip didn't see a ring on the waiter's large hand, a hand better suited, she thinks, for clutching pistons or sheering sheep than decanting wine. But she wonders what she really knows in the first place. Nor does she have a ring of her own to see. Does it matter? Does she really need a ring? Pip doesn't think rings are necessary, really. But Mr. Khakis Crotch is another matter. Did he check? Is she someone a man like her waiter checks for such things as rings? She got no hint of anything from him other than the need to nearly shout in order to be heard over the rushing creek in the gorge below. And, how could she know? All she had seen was a button-fly. And a hand that didn't want Pip to go hungry or thirsty. And when she looked for a face all she had seen had been orange blotches that disintegrated the way a receding hand that bids farewell grows smaller and smaller.

Pip turns a page, then another. Still no resolution to the open-ended parens. She blinks. This discord, this disquiet, she realizes, will stay a while.

Orange Tree Dog

I was playing catch with Orange Tree Dog when my mom pulled into the driveway after work the day Raina died. Mom sighed and dropped the car into Park and looked at me with distant eyes. Then she lowered her head and heaved herself out of the car and hobbled toward the house.

Mom said she had these floating bone chips in her ankle that she needed to rearrange into proper alignment in order to avoid limping or wincing so much. It didn't help that for her job she needed to walk around a lot, going door to door, counting the people, and for her night job, too, waiting tables at a restaurant. Sometimes rest and ice helped, but most of the time she managed the pain with ankle exercises—drawing air doodles with the tips of her toes— and meditating with her jade plant.

It was about dinnertime. I threw the stick one more time and Orange Tree Dog grabbed it and ran off down the street. I always liked to watch her run. Like the wind, even for an old dog. I was eleven, but that dog was much, much older. Between forty and fifty years old in people years. That's three to four hundred in dog years. The dog's occupancy of the house she lived at pre-dated every single resident on this end of town, and no one in the neighborhood could ever remember her not being around. She was always included in the sale of the house, just like you would expect an oak or a maple or a fence to be included. The home owners all had varying reasons for leaving the dog behind—one sustained a major head injury, one family moved overseas, and so on—and in the end, the reality was that after so many years, the house was more hers than any human occupant's.

The most recent residents of Orange Tree Dog's house were a pair of older women, Raina and Rachel, who had lived there together for about five years, along with that dog, who napped beneath a blossoming mock orange shrub the size of a tree out in the front yard. I was convinced that the power of this huge shrub's sweet-smelling magic is what allowed the dog to live so long.

Raina and Rachel were pretty cool. Rachel was a painter and Raina taught music. They threw open their windows, loosing the exotic aromas of what they were cooking to wander down the neighborhood sidewalks, and they hosted garden parties and recitals in their big back yard. Everyone was invited. We'd sit around, throw sticks and balls for Orange Tree Dog, try their interesting foods, and listen to her students play violin and cello. Raina and Rachel wore their hair up in clumps with these fancy chopsticks poking through, and walked around in colorful flowing clothes. Having them live here was like having another part of another place altogether right down the street.

I never heard what was wrong with Raina. Just that she had to go to the hospital more and more often, and soon she wasn't able to teach or hold more parties or make their end of the street smell like some other country. And when Mom pulled into the driveway that day, I could tell there was something else wrong beyond fatigue and poor bone-chip alignment. She shook her head and said that we were going to make banana bread for Rachel. Rachel had been packing up the house for over a month, Mom said, and a new buyer was waiting to move in. I nodded and wondered if the new buyer would mind if I played with Orange Tree Dog after they got settled.

I carried the groceries into the house while Mom got ready to go to her next job. I wiped down the chipped green Formica and put away the groceries and got to making something for us to eat.

I fired up the stove and replaced the soft brown bananas on the counter with the fresh green hard ones. Mom was always aging bananas in a sunny kitchen window. I'd arrange the brown ones in the freezer into nice, neat rows, one nestled within another, before they rotted entirely if we didn't have enough time to make banana bread, and for a while there, I'm pretty sure we always had a dozen or so frozen bananas waiting to be thawed out for that loaf of sympathy. Mom was gone a lot for her jobs, but she always found a way to take time to see to folks in pain, or someone in need of a slice of kindness. Even so, it seemed there were lots of times when there weren't enough bananas to meet demand. But Mom tried.

School was only about ten blocks away, so I always walked. I liked to arrive early to chat with my buddy, Donelle, one of the school's janitors. She had white hair and black eyes and heavy red-rimmed glasses. Her eyes were always so wide, like she was constantly surprised, and she had a loud laugh and big teeth. I once heard of a school in the next town over where the janitor became the school's guidance counselor. I believed it because Donelle was a person like that. I told her all about my mom being always away at work, my mean teachers, the crooked and broken stone sidewalk pavers that led all the way to the school, and throwing rocks at the neighbors' cats because they ate up the songbirds in our yard. Donelle listened to everything I had to say. Some days we'd sit on the high brick wall that bordered the playground and eat lunch together. She always had a pickle sandwich and a piece of fruit and a chunk of cheese. It was nice to sit outside. We'd peer over our knees at the ant mounds below and eat, bumping our heels against the brick wall and tell each other we were dangling our feet off the edge of the Earth.

One day, I noticed that Donelle was eating a banana. I asked her if she ever made banana bread. She rolled her eyes and made a face. "Sounds pretty exotic," she groaned. Then she chirped in a silly way, "I prefer eating to baking," and popped what was left of the banana into her mouth.

We laughed and then I told her Mom and I were going to make banana bread for Rachel, the partner of Raina, our neighbor who just died.

"Did you know Raina?" I asked.

Donelle shook her head. "No," she said. "I did not." She reached over and touched me on the back. "But I am sorry."

Just then Orange Tree Dog padded up to us for a visit. I hopped off the wall and grabbed a stick and threw it for her.

"Mom says this dog is about forty years old. I think she's crazy."

The dog brought the stick back and we wrestled around for a while until finally she let go and I threw it for her again. She picked up the stick and continued on her way. That's how Orange Tree Dog was: Visit, play, move on. She was a great dog . . . always with places to be. And she had this way of angling down the street that made it seem as though she was about to veer in a different direction than the one her body was actually headed. It was the funniest thing.

Donelle shook her head and smiled after the dog left. "Your mother is not crazy," she said, and picked at her teeth. "Everyone knows that dog is sixty if it's a day."

Mom said that in addition to sending Rachel banana bread, she'd like to germinate a plant clipping for her, too. "Something from around here to remember us by. She can have it on her patio. Then she'll always have her old neighborhood with her." She looked at me squarely. She knew that I knew my part of town better than any kid around, that in my head I possessed a mental mapping of the location of every apple tree and raspberry bush from the train tracks behind our house, down to the river, and up to the very busy Dupin Avenue. (I was never allowed to cross Dupin Avenue by myself.) Mom continued to look at me. Did I have any suggestions?

I was still thinking of Orange Tree Dog. "What about that blossoming orange tree? Then she'd have something to remember Orange Tree Dog by, too."

Seemed pretty obvious to me, but Mom went instantly quiet like she hadn't considered this. Maybe because Orange Tree Dog's house was located just a bit out of the way in the opposite direction of where we both went every day: Me to school, and her to her jobs. Maybe because she had so many other things to think about. I don't know. Mom often acted like she was thinking about something that was really far away, or that happened a long time ago.

She pulled her hand from her mouth and started to speak after a minute. Her voice caught, and she stopped herself and reached for her jade plant instead.

I walked by Orange Tree Dog's house the next day to ask about the tree. A very large man with a huge beard that covered his neck sat on the front porch. A fluorescent yellow sleeveless shirt that showed off his big bare arms stretched tight over his round belly. He wore faded blue jeans and black work boots, and had bushy black hair that made it look like he was always hot.

"Did you know her," I asked.

"Know who?" His eyes seemed to disappear into his face when he spoke.

"Rachel."

"Rachel?" He looked confused. "No, I don't know no Rachel." He looked at me suspiciously. Everyone around town seemed to know Rachel and Raina, except for anyone I happened to talk to.

"She lived here," I said. "Before you. So I was thinking I'd grow a little tree for her." I pointed at the mock orange shrub.

"That?" he asked, surprised. "Just some overgrown bush…"

"Something to remember this by," I said, and held my arms out wide. The yard and garden beyond were beautiful. I looked at the magical tree again. The powerful sweet fragrance from the tree's huge white blossoms encircled the entire yard, and almost made me dizzy.

"Fine," he said, still sitting on his porch. "You can break off a little piece and try to grow one of yer own if ya wanna." He gestured to the tree and shook his head.

I thanked him, and realized that I'd forgotten my pocketknife. I patted all my pockets to be sure. Probably in the washing machine, again. Normally, I would have just broken off a few branches, but I was afraid I'd peel off too much bark and hurt the tree. This guy was pretty scary.

I shrugged and said I would be back with a knife in a couple of days.

"Well," he said, and cleared his throat. "Ya better put some hustle on that, then."

"Why?" I'd already started to walk away, and when I looked back, I had to shield my eyes from the sun. All I could see was a dark, bushy silhouette with a glowing shirt talking to me. It was more than a little spooky.

"Cuttin it down," he said, exasperated, like I should know. "Next coupla weeks."

I squinted harder at him.

"Need room for my RV."

I blinked. An army? I thought. Wow. I thought about my mom and her job of counting people. I stepped closer and asked, "Has anyone been by to count you yet?"

His body shook like he had no idea what I was talking about.

"Count me? Wuddya mean?"

"Ja. My mom goes around to all the houses and counts the people."

The man looked at me and tilted his head. "Nope," he said. "Just moved in." He pointed over his shoulder toward the house with his thumb.

Finally, I said, "Okay," and left.

I wandered home, stepping from sidewalk stone to sidewalk stone, dodging the wide, grassy gaps between—hot lava—with this new news. This man, who was maybe waiting to be counted, him and his army, was going to chop down that big flowery fragrant shrub. Occasionally I stopped to inspect an earthworm that avoided the hot lava by stretching out on a damp, shady paver, or to eat a handful of mulberries. I arrived home with hands and lips splotched blue and purple, like the uneven stones.

Mom was meditating when I got there. She always sat with her big old jade plant. Sometimes she touched the leaves. Something about tracing the edges of those succulent leaves that seemed to take on her pain. Sometimes I thought I could see the plant tremble when Mom reached for it.

I washed my hands extra long—Mom always worried that I'd get berry stains on the upholstery, even though I actually didn't like having messy fingers anyway—and told Mom that the man who bought Orange Tree Dog's house was going to chop down the mock orange shrub.

"That beautiful bush?" she said. "Why, who would do such a thing?" She paused and shook her head and grasped a different leaf. The plant winced. "And, *what* on earth for?"

"Says he needs room for an army." I blinked and looked around the kitchen for a snack. The bananas on the countertop were still pretty green. "Are we going to make banana bread now," I asked. Mom was still looking at me curiously. I could tell she wanted more information. Maybe she was calculating how long it would take to count them all, the hairy man and his entire army. "Well," I said, "he says he's gonna put them all where the orange tree is now." I swung open the freezer door and peeked inside. "Set up a bunch of tents for them, maybe?" Mom aligned bone chips in her ankle by spelling out something with the tips of her toes. Inside the freezer, my frozen and black bananas were still lined up in neat rows.

I took several pieces of Rachel's banana bread batch to school the next day. I gave one to my teacher, one to the teacher I hoped to get the next year, and later gave one to Donelle out on the edge of the Earth.

Donelle thanked me and nodded and chewed. "Nice and moist," she said. "Usually banana bread is so dry."

I nodded a thanks and chewed on my piece.

"You doin anything fun this weekend?" she said.

I had no idea. "Probably clean the house and do laundry," I said, and paused to swallow. "Maybe cook." Donelle laughed but stopped when I added that if Mom wasn't at work, she'd probably be icing her bad leg.

"Oh," Donelle said. Her face fell a little. "Sounds like a lot."

I didn't say anything.

"What does your mother do for a living?" She looked concerned. "Is she a carpenter, or like a welder or sumthin?"

"Nope," I said. "For one of her jobs, Mom's a people counter."

"A people counter?" Donelle seemed confused. "Who does she count people for?" I could sense her wry smile.

"She works for a company called Census. They go around and count all the people that live in all the towns."

"Ah," she said. "Now I get it." She stretched. "Sorry buddy," she said, and reached over to rub my back. "You hang in there."

My legs dangled from the edge of the Earth. I tapped my heels together while I chewed. "It's fine," I said. "I'll make do." Then I smiled at her and asked about her plans for the weekend. She seemed surprised that I would ask.

She showed her big teeth and said, "Well, me, I'm goin fishin. Me an my boyfriend."

"Oh, wow. Whatcha fishin for?"

"Crappies," she said. "He knows this one spot where this one reservoir is full of huge crappies. I guess the DNR checked and said there were more crappies there than anywhere else in the area. Everyone was surprised because no one knew that there were even any fish in there in the first place."

"Really," I said. "How . . . do they count the fish?" I looked around. Seemed like the school bell ending the lunch recess should have rung by now. We bumped our heels against the wall a few times.

"They electrocute the water, and all the fish float up. Then the agents count them all while they're stunned and can't swim away."

I swallowed and felt myself go light and numb. Shocking the water to count the fish. Was this how Mom counted the people? I closed my eyes and saw Mom calmly fire a canister of sleeping gas through the window of a house, climb in after it, and clinically record a count on a notepad of all the passed out people inside.

"He wanted to take his camper to go somewhere else," she said, "but I told him to sell it, the camper. That we don't need that ugly old thing. You should see it." She shook her head and took a drink from a water bottle. "So," she said, still with some of Rachel's banana bread in her mouth, "we're just gonna head out in his truck where we can pitch a tent by that reservoir and do some fishin." She chewed more bread. "For my birthday."

"Camper?"

"Yep. Said he'd put a big ole 'for sale' sign on it." Donelle chewed. I watched her jaw muscles jump. "Promised to take me somewhere nice when it gets cold out with the money he gets."

A boyfriend? I tried to imagine what he could look like.

"Sure hope we go somewhere warm," Donelle was saying.

All possible images of the boyfriend drifted from view. Donelle was sitting with me now, eating the bread I made from frozen bananas with my mom. I chewed on my piece. Donelle was right: This batch came out nice and moist. I continued to chew, and nodded, and for a while we both just looked around at stuff. The sky, the treetops, the crooked and misaligned sidewalk pavers and the ragged grassy gaps in between. Those bugged me. Then I remembered that she said it was her birthday.

"Well, happy birthday!" I said. I knew enough not to ask how old she was, so I didn't. But I did look her up and down a couple of times. I'm pretty sure she noticed because she snorted and said, "You wonderin how old I am?"

I shook my head and slid off our edge of the Earth. Shaking my head was a lie, and she knew it.

"Oh, it's okay," she said. "Everyone does. It's normal." She smiled at me big again. I coughed. "Let's just say that I'm younger than our friend over there." Just then Orange Tree Dog padded past us, careening the way she did, but moving really fast and with a determined look about her like she was on some kind of mission.

Mom got home pretty late that day, even for her. It happened sometimes that the people counting took longer than usual. And that meant more time for me to play in the yard with friends and Orange Tree Dog, if she was around. (She wasn't.) I knew I should have assumed that Mom would be home any minute, and been inside making dinner, but sometimes it's nice to play outside like it's not a school night.

Once inside, I started rice and began to cut vegetables for a stir-fry. Mom sat next to her jade and watched me for a while. She didn't mention the time, or dinner being late.

"Did you grab some clippings?" She glanced around the kitchen, and leaned from her chair to look out onto the porch, probably for a vase that contained the blossoms I was meant to pot for Rachel.

I stopped cutting and reached for the green beans. Mom propped her leg on the footrest and looked over at me. I knew that this was my cue to fetch an icepack.

Rummaging in the freezer gave me a minute to think. Easy answer was No, I had not grabbed the blossoms. Orange Tree Dog's house was sorta out of the way from ours, so Mom would have been cool with me saying that I didn't make it over there. But the truth was that the man now living there scared me, and I wasn't sure why, and I didn't feel like trying to explain that.

"No," I said. "Just stayed here after school."

"Well, just don't forget about it," Mom said. Her eyes darted up at me.

Then her eyes got soft as I pressed the icepack onto her ankle. "Thank you sweetheart." She tipped her head back against the headrest and murmured, "Poor Rachel." I chopped vegetables for the stir-fry and watched her eyes close and her fingertips stroke a jade leaf. The rice wasn't close to being done. The jade did what it could. Mom needed to leave in less than an hour.

The next time I sat with Donelle, she said something about Orange Tree Dog disappearing. I was staring at the sidewalk pavers that ran from the street corner up below my feet, trying to get the edges to line up again, this time out of the corner of one eye by closing the other.

"Haven't seen it around much," she said. "If at all."

This jolted me from my trance. I hadn't seen the dog in a while, either. How could I have not noticed?

"Do you think she ran away?" I yelped, and tumbled off the wall. Me, falling from the edge of the Earth. I landed heavily, but quickly rose to a knee and tied a shoe to leave, trying to make it look like I fell on purpose.

Donelle ignored this. "No clue," she said. "All I know is no one's seen it last coupla days."

"Oh no," I wailed. I knew right then that something was terribly wrong. I remembered how she trotted past us so fast just a few days before, like she seriously needed to be somewhere else. I hadn't seen her since.

I started to run away, but Donelle called out and stopped me. "Hey!" There was a piercing urgency to her voice, the way adults get, like when you're about to touch something that's really hot, or step out into traffic, and her eyes were even more wild and surprised-looking than usual. "School? Remember? Can't leave the grounds til end of day…"

I got a funny taste in my mouth, like you do right before you're about to puke. I turned and sprinted away.

It didn't take long to reach Orange Tree Dog's house. I came to a skidding stop on the other side of the street. I must have looked like a cartoon character, screeching up within a cloud of dust. Orange Tree House Man sat, reclined on his front steps like the last time, all big and bushy and scary and tight-yellow-shirted. I recovered from my abrupt stop and walked slowly over to where the mock orange should have swayed in the breeze. Instead there was a school-bus-sized camper vehicle. It was a faded creamy white, with rusted-out holes around the tires and a mis-matching brown door spray-painted darker in spots. A crooked TV antenna bent over a side, and one of the windows was partially broken out.

There was small sheet of chipped plywood with "4 SALE" spray-painted the same color as the camper door leaning against the front bumper.

The man looked up at me. I had no air to speak. He shook his head the way adults do. "Told ya I was gonna cut the fucker down," he said.

I didn't really see him. The wood shavings from chainsaws were still curly and fresh and bright beneath the huge vehicle. I tried to imagine Mom driving such a thing, or seeing my face when I heard the f-word. My ears started to ring.

I was kicking myself on the insides for not bringing along a knife the day I first asked the man about taking a clipping when I finally remembered the dog.

"The dog..." I squeaked.

"Omar?" he said, and shrugged. "Dunno. He took off coupla days ago when we fired up the chainsaw." He sniffed. "Prolly gun shy, is all."

"Omar?" I couldn't think of anything else to say. After all these years, I had no idea what the dog's name was. I guessed that she had outlived a number of owners, and thus a number of names.

"Ja. Named him Omar one day. Seemed to like it."

"Huh." I looked at the camper again. The bent antenna was distracting and attention-calling at the same time. I wanted to straighten it. The camper itself seemed tired and looked like it probably smelled bad on the inside. Then my mind went back to Orange Tree Dog. Omar. What? I couldn't imagine calling her anything other than Orange Tree Dog. And the thought of her running away or getting hurt sickened me.

I walked home and kept looking back at the shrubs. Or the big ugly camper that used to be the shrubs. The thought of that made me sick, too. Those gorgeous shrubs. The magic of those bright white blooms, so sweet they made you dizzy. Gone.

I slowed my pace. The 4 SALE sign. A flash of understanding overtook me. This was Donelle's boyfriend. My ears began to ring louder. Her idea to sell the camper. The mock orange. Orange Tree Dog leaving. Donelle was behind it all. Now I was sure I would puke. But I turned back to the man, Donelle's boyfriend, instead.

He raised one of his big hairy arms at me to wave goodbye, showing his black underarm. It was like a tunnel of darkness that pathed right into a nothingness in the middle of his body. I didn't know what to do. I realized that I was starting to cry. But I waved back at the man, then turned to walk the rest of the way home.

I paused and stared down at the fronds of clipped grass between the berry-stained sidewalk stones. There was no hot lava today, so it was safe to step between them, and for earthworms to crawl there. I closed my eyes and inhaled deeply. My breath caught. I hoped Mom would be by his place any minute now to zap the guy like one of Donelle's crappies, or hit him with sleeping gas for later counting.

Maybe Mom could zap Donelle, too, while she was at it.

I opened my eyes and was struck by a slender tree limb dangling in front of my face. I glanced around. A softness had crept into the air. Mulberries. I plucked a handful of berries, then another, and ate every one of them, one after the other, and didn't even check for rot spots or bugs.

The sky was turning pink, and the soft air pressed in on me. Orange Tree Dog was gone.

A teary sigh chuffed from my lungs, and I was glad that the man with the hole pathing through his body into the nothingness inside him had gone back into his house and couldn't see. I thought about Donelle telling me about going fishing with this guy, her boyfriend, and how now, after this, the edge of the Earth would always be everywhere, and especially unavoidable.

Raina came to mind. She would have lingered in this moment of soft, pink air, too. It was like I could see her, standing on the stone walkway beneath this tree, her long black hair, light flowery dress. She would have raised a hand, her long fingers gently cupping one of the blossoms, and turned it toward Rachel at her side. And I decided, in that moment that Rachel would have smiled, to cut off a few small branches in bloom, one at a time.

At least I'd remembered my pocket knife.

The soft evening air followed me into our house. Mom was meditating with her jade, leg propped up. The pink sky was purple and drowsy now, the hour somehow much later than it should have been. I snipped the ends of the mulberry stems and slipped them inside a glass jar I filled with water. Mom stirred.

I turned the jar on the counter for her to see.

She stroked a jade leaf and looked up at me. She regarded the branches sticking up from that jar, her eyes tracing up and down along a line on the edge of each not-mock-orange blossom. Her ankle crackled as the tip of her big toe traced part of the alphabet. She looked up at me. The soft evening air filled the walls to the corners.

"Perfect," Mom said.

I Prefer You in Spanish

I prefer you in Spanish, she says. She sets down her glass. So, please, she says, in Spanish, Don't speak to me in English. She doesn't wait for him to say anything. Thank you, she says, and exhales loudly.

They fell in love in Salamanca. It didn't take long. They were meant for each other.

She is from Connecticut. He is from somewhere in Michigan. Her parents are from Madrid, and his mother is from Lima. She wants to live in Rio de Janeiro, and he insists that Lake Superior will never let him go.

The college-age boy smiles at the girl across the table from him at the outdoor café of the Plaza Mayor in Salamanca, and pours beer. He taps the heels of his hard shoes on the centuries-old stone floor beneath his feet. Walls of the enclosed plaza throb a sandstone golden gleam at the ancient city's center. A waiter dressed in black bearing a platter of bowls filled with aromatic salads, and plates heaped with toasted tomato-and-basil sandwiches dodges a pair of darting children.

It's your accent, she says. All 'Yaah' and 'Geez' and '*Soooper!*'

She wears a light cream blouse. Petals of muted red roses arc in tight stitches across a dark brown skirt. She recrosses her legs and looks around the Plaza Mayor. A discarded page of newsprint tumbles across the stone sections of the plaza and becomes wedged in the legs of a folding chair resting against a table at the next café. Students waiting in clusters pace about beneath the main clock tower beyond, a customary meeting place.

You make me sound Canadian, he grumbles.

Yes! she says. You're practically Canada anyway. North Dakota. Manitoba. Michigan. Iowa. What difference does it make? the girl says. She moves her hands a lot when she speaks. You're all Ontario to us!

He notices a girl with shiny hair walk by. She wears a red skirt and a yellow sleeveless blouse.

The girl across from him scoops her black bangs aside and nods to the passing yellow sleeveless. She's pretty . . . she says, also watching. She raises an eyebrow in a way that drives the boy wild.

Yes, he says. He clears his throat. She is.

The pretty girl in a yellow top and red skirt disappears behind the pillar of a wide Baroque arch. He looks back at the girl across from him. Yellow-top girl was indeed pretty. Though the boy knows, in his heart, that he will never know anyone as beautiful to him as this green-eyed girl sitting across from him now.

She's got nuthin on ya, he says. You, my dear, he says, are gorgeous. Stunning.

The girl snorts. There you go again, she says, in Spanish. With that damn accent. I'm begging you, she says. I adore you, but please. Lose the English. I . . . I just don't like you . . . in *English*. Sorry. I just don't.

He folds his arms and looks around for their waiter, then back at the arch. His beer is empty and the pretty girl in red and yellow is still gone.

That, and you're just so much less interesting in English, she says, in Spanish.

They are quiet for a while.

Same thing doesn't happen to you, the boy says. You don't suddenly become some dullard just for speaking your native tongue.

Spanish?

No, silly.

English? Maybe, she says, and frowns. I don't know. I think about things in Spanish about as often as I do English. What if I told you Spanish is my native tongue?

Bah. It's not. It can't be. You grew up—

My parents are Spanish, she says. *Spaniards*. From—

—grew up in Connecticut.

—Madrid, Spain, in fact, she says. People, she says, folding her arms across her chest, of Spain. She gives a resolute nod.

Doesn't matter, he says, in English. Yer nuthin but East Coast. He stares at her for an extra moment and smiles. It's on yer breath.

They pass the University and cross the cobbled Puente Romano, millennia old, and stare into the slow current of the wide Río Tormes.

And the things you talk about in Spanish, she says, in Spanish, are just so much more interesting.

Yeah? the boy says. His insides burst with delight. He continues in Spanish. What sorts of things?

Yes, she insists. Music. Geopolitics. Race. Art—

Art? he says, and scoffs. Art. I am *so* over artists.

The girl's green eyes gleam, and she raises an eyebrow the way she does. Really? Why?

Narcissists. All of them.

What makes you say that? She turns her head quickly to look at the river.

I didn't hear that either, he says.

Hear what?

That thing that you didn't hear that you just turned your head to look for.

She looks at the river again, then back at the boy. She shrugs.

Yeah, he says, I don't get it, either. There's something not quite right about this river. It's like a motion sickness . . . that comes from over . . . there, he says. The boy nods to the far river bank.

The girl nods, too. I suspect, she says, that the Romans felt the same way . . . Which is why they built this bridge to span it . . . rather than wade in to it . . . The girl continues to stare. Her eyes scan the gentle current for the odd thing that neither of them heard. She extends an arm to him at her side. You noticed it, too, she says, distantly, and still reaching, absently.

I did, he says, and takes her hand. Her fingers are long and cool and smooth. His hand is strong and hard and clean. You don't suppose, he says, and lowers his voice to switch to English, that this river is . . . *haunted?*

The word *haunted* breaks her trance. She blinks and turns to look at him. That wasn't so bad, she says. When you speak conspiratorially, your English becomes bearable, she says. She rolls her tongue behind her teeth in thought. She turns her head to the river again and says, Though I must say I prefer *encantado* to *haunted*. Has more to do with spirits dwelling within, rather than a disturbing—or a disturbed—presence.

Late July in Central Spain. The boy and the girl decide to travel south to the coast at Cádiz. Hit the beach before the fall session at University. Make some cultural-touristy stops along the way.

They take an *Expreso* train to Madrid. There is nothing *Expreso* about it. The boy falls asleep reading *Faust* in Spanish. She eats dry jamón serrano with Zamorano cheese and dark olives and bits of Spanish rolls. Leaden clouds cycle through the windowpanes atop the undulating warp of sparse plains. The sleeping boy's stomach rises and falls. The train presses down and thrums drowsily upon the rails. He breathes through his nose. *Faust* lays tipped, pages bent, across his thigh. She watches the open grassy fields swish past, and the filtered sunlight dabble shadow and beams along the edge of his high cheek bone, down to where his clavicle disappears beneath a beige linen shirt collar.

When he wakes he explains that reading in Spanish makes him sleepy faster than reading in English. She nods.

The grasses cease, like a yanked curtain. Madrid is instant city.

The girl has family in Madrid. He has never been here. Eventually, she says, from a room with peeling plaster walls in a low-rate hostel near the Prado, I need to meet up with them. Inés has a nice place, she says. She taps the boy's knee. We should go, she says.

The room is hot. Madrid is loud. The boy looks up, drowsy. Inés?

My aunt, the girl says. Dad's sister.

In Toledo, the former capital of the Taifa Kingdom of al-Andalus, they stroll Visigoth walls, Moorish Mosques, and gaze at the massive Gothic Cathedral. A Tarot card reader works the Cathedral steps. The girl begs the boy to have the woman read his cards. He insists that the cards never flip in his favor.

Then you have nothing to lose, the girl says.

The woman spreads her fingertips and snaps the cards and raises her eyebrows. She says her family is from Melilla, in the north of Africa.

But I grew up in Fermoselle, she says to the boy. Zamora. Western Spain, she says.

The boy nods vaguely.

Where the Río Tormes ends, the woman says. Her eyes widen and she tugs at a gold loop that pierces an ear and adjusts a ring on the hand holding the cards. Where the Tormes ends, she repeats, in an affected voice.

The girl elbows the boy. They look into each other, and feel the churn of their haunted-river moment on the Puente Romano in Salamanca.

Fine, he says.

A serious look fills the woman's clear encantado eyes. She pulls her dark hair aside and cuts the cards. The thick cards do not flip in the boy's favor. He shakes his head and looks at the girl. The woman's deep eyes flare with a flicker of darkness. She explains that a disappointment, like a falling object splashing down, is soon headed his way. The girl explodes into tears and pulls the boy into a bar.

It's hot and dark inside the bar opposite the Cathedral. The ceilings are low and the windows are pulled shut. Dense cigarette smoke makes him cough. The bartender stirs a rabbit stew simmering in a kettle at the end of the bar. The boy tells the girl that Vargas Llosa wrote an extensive novel around a bar in Lima called La Catedral. A novel that posits its core question in the opening paragraph: At what point did el Perú come to be so fucked?

Carajo, he says, and coughs. El Perú is still fucked.

She is still weepy but nods and laughs. Good boy, she sniffs. That's how I prefer you. Even if it be vulgar, may it be in Spanish.

They catch a south-bound train that night.

In Córdoba, intervocalic consonants of Castilian Spanish disappear. The boy laughs at the local accent. He has never heard people who speak like this live and in living flesh. He laughs again. The boy is built like his Finnish father, but speaks like his limeña mom. So he gets away with it. The green-eyed girl is the entirety of Iberia in a champagne flute, and so she gets away with everything.

In Córdoba, they lose the planet. Historic Caliphate, a masterpiece of al-Andalus architecture. Tight cobblestone ways twist beneath the twitter of songbirds, a drunken embrace of fragrant flowers, and immaculate courtyards of dazzling white walls, indigo trim, Arabic tiles, and balconies heaped with flowers in bloom. A passing local recognizes their look of awe and tells them to return next May for the Fiesta de los Patios. All the private patios will be open to the public, he says. He raps a locked wrought-iron gate with a walking stick. Like this one, he says, and peers inside. His accent is thick and steeped with millennia of pride and the good luck of having lived his entire life in the exact center of the universe.

We should come back for that, the girl says, leaning against a wall to enjoy a moment of shade.

In Córdoba, the boy clears his throat. You don't tell these people to cool it on their accent, he says, in Spanish. He removes his hand from the wrought-iron gate, and looks at her. His eyes narrow. This accent, he says, and extends his arms. Easily as absurd as mine in English.

The girl gasps. She understands that he is not joking. She shrugs.

Well, she says. It's how they talk here. They can't help being where they're from. She looks away.

In Córdoba, the boy tells the girl to fuck off. In English.

In Sevilla, the temperature never drops below 100 degrees Fahrenheit. The girl drags baguette slices through drippings of fresh olive oils and drinks tall bottles of beer. Dangling legs of aged serrano ham perspire globules of fat that pat, heavily, onto the bar. Crumbled cheese smears between her fingertips.

A bartender asks, in a purring voice, How is the food? The girl raises her eyes to him. She starts to sigh, but this man is merely doing his job. She lifts her chin and wipes her forehead with the back of a hand. It occurs to her in that moment that she can taste none of any of this. The girl sniffs, then smiles. Her Spanish social graces provide a response that contents the barman. He nods and leaves.

At night, the ancient city's brick walls breathe heat. It's like sleeping in a kiln. By day, she endures, alone, four-hour siestas and a towering sun and no shade. In the morning she drinks steamed coffee and eats hot soft rolls and wanders a cathedral built atop a mosque razed by Christians. She shakes her head. The comments the boy would have about all of this.

She's not certain what the boy is doing all this time. He doesn't speak. His eyes remain vacant. The summer skies are sultry and gray, the air a yellowish green all around.

Late afternoon, cobalt blue skies slide in and replace the yellowish-green with a buzzing golden glitter.

The next day, she invites the boy out. At least eat something, she says.

They split a whole spit-roasted chicken, a long length of bread, a bottle of water, a half kilo of red grapes, and two liters of beer. The heat is oppressive. Still the boy does not speak. He sleeps most of the following day. The girl washes her long black hair and her blouse in the room sink. She watches the boy sleep. She leans back and reads *El País*, topless, while her hair and her blouse dry in the sun.

They arrive late to Cádiz. The jefe at the hostel doesn't allow unmarried couples to share a room. The boy says fine with him, the girl can have the room. He starts to leave, but the jefe tells him it's not safe in the streets at this hour. He eyes the boy up and down. Even for you, he says. He allows the boy to sleep in the kitchen at a reduced rate.

The doña of the hostel, the real jefe-in-chief, it turns out, steps on the boy asleep on the kitchen floor before first light. She screams and he wakes and hollers and minutes later they both drink coffee and laugh and laugh while she makes churros and chocolate and cracks eggs and chops herbs and potatoes for Spanish tortillas.

The doña minces onions and tells the boy about German tourists. You look German, she says, and points a knife at the boy. Her hands never stop moving. The boy stirs. The doña speaks in shrieks. The knife in her hand cuts in sharp snaps.

The boy leans back and inhales deeply and folds his arms and stretches and blinks. The doña chatters. The dogs in the alleyways of our city here, she is saying, in her sweet and tender voice, fuck constantly. You'll see, she says, it's all they do is fuck. But please don't be disgusted, thanks, it's just their nature, the pobrecitos.

A hot day roils in the pre-dawn haze. Cádiz is not Upper Michigan. The boy rises to his feet. Time to be an adult about this girl thing. So what if she doesn't like his accent. She's mostly kidding anyway. And she obviously likes *you*, he thinks.

The boy leaves to wake the girl, hopes to surprise her with his news of fresh Spanish tortillas and churros and thick drinking chocolate. She opens her eyes and all at once tells him all what she smells. He watches her electric eyes, the delightful delight of her surprise.

The boy returns. The doña has not stopped talking. The boy raises his coffee cup. The sun is all the way up. There's no stopping the doña.

There's not a lot to do in Cádiz. The beaches are hot and strong winds off the Atlantic blow sand and trash all around. The museums open late and close early for the long siesta. They eat another entire chicken and wander the port and wish they hadn't drunk so much beer.

A flat cargo ship pulls into port. A man on the deck throws an American football across the channel to the boy, end over end. The man on the boat does not know how to throw a football. The boy flags down the ball before it bounds off the edge of the pier. He looks down at the ball in his hands, traces a thumb over the official NFL seal.

Men on the ship stretch their arms and beckon for the ball. It's not clear what language they speak. The boy shrugs. Go on, the girl urges, in English. Throw it back.

The boy turns to the girl. They stand in each other's gaze. She nods. The girl gives him a small smile. Go on, she repeats, again in English. Throw it back, she whispers. She twitches her head at the ship. The vessel glides by, deceptively fast. Her eyes widen. Hurry, she pleads.

The boy loosens his neck and snaps a tight spiral across the open water in an effortless arc to the men in the boat. The ball bounces off a scramble of lunging hands. It was a perfect pass. The ball careens and tips overboard and falls in a slow plummet into the oil-slicked brine of the port.

Carajo, the boy mutters.

The girl exhales and pulls her fingers through her black hair. She recalls the Tarot card reader in Toledo. The woman from where the Tormes ends, her flickering encantado eyes, the fortune she uttered, the odd squirm on her insides when the woman said *Tormes*. And the boy's strong hand she used to steady herself on that bridge in Salamanca, and later his soft eyes when she told him all about all what she smelled the moment she first awoke here in Cádiz.

The boy curses and laughs and waves his arms at the men on the receding ship. The men groan and laugh and hold their heads and wave back. The girl laughs, too.

The girl comes from Connecticut. He is from somewhere in Michigan. Her parents are from Madrid, and the boy's mother hails from Lima. They recently fell in love in Salamanca, where she told him about preferring him in Spanish. Yet she's just realized, watching an American football bob and drift away harmlessly in the oily brine of the Puerto de Cádiz, that in spite of herself, what she really prefers is him.

Dumplings

God, how I hate this dog. Small, dumpy, and loud, Mrs. Bagsley is one of them constant yipper types.

So, just now she comes steaming and slobbering into my yard and before I know what I'm doing, I blow her head off with my Ruger P90, *foomp*. More weapon than required for such a runt, but she didn't suffer. Small animals die fast if you do it right.

Silencers are beautiful and awesome, but there is still a bit of a mess to clean up. Now what? Certainly Edna next door will find her missing at any moment. No matter how vile or inbred anyone may have found that animal to be, I'm guessing that blowing its head off isn't exactly neighborly.

"Mrs. Bagsley?" Edna calls out from around the corner, "Where are you pumpkin-butt?"

OK, now this is bad. Edna is about to charge over here in her ragged skirt and pilled lime sweater to ask if I've seen her precious.

I slip Mrs. Bagsley into a plastic bag and sneak inside my kitchen to skin her like a rabbit. I've just decided we're having soup tonight. By the time Edna comes banging inside my back door, Mrs. Bagsley is already in the pot, and I've started in on slicing the onions, carrots, celery, and garlic. The key to a good broth is to cook it slowly and to allow the core of your stock—chicken, beef, or in this case, a former Shi-Tzu—to simmer for a couple hours. It's a luxury for sure, but once the meat is fully cooked, you end up with an exceptional base and an animal that is perfect for making soup. You then just need to bone it, and even that's not necessary, really.

I start to plop in the sliced vegetables. "Why no, Edna, I have not seen Mrs. Bagsley." She correctly knows that something is wrong. Or, at the very least, that something is not quite right, and even the black flats that groan across her meaty feet seem to echo her distress.

"I saw her walk into your yard." She glances around. "And you were outside, too. Smells good," she adds, nodding at the stove.

"Thanks . . . Dunno." I give the pot a stir. "Maybe she waddled over to the Oostermans'." I point their way with my chin, and finally she leaves so I can catch my breath.

This is bad. Very bad. I murdered my neighbor's dog, I lied to her about it, and now I'm stirring the thing atop my stove. I'm too capable to behave like this. The doctor said that I'd be forever changed, and that I'd eventually adapt, but . . .

Anyway, so I grab a can of Nails Ale from the fridge and wash down three prescribed caplets, and pace around. I need to fix this.

Mrs. Bagsley, meanwhile, is now coming to a boil and needs more peppercorns. And a bay leaf and a quick stir. I set down my beer and walk around the yard while the dog, partially covered, simmers on low.

2:47 Monday afternoon. Everyone in the 'hood at work. Technically, I'm working too. Upstairs in my home office the cursor on my computer monitor reaches out and blinks for me, bitter and forlorn, stranded at the beginning of the same line of text as an hour ago. Meanwhile, I've taken to shooting up my neighbors' pets. I close my eyes and massage my temples, and head back to the house.

I return and Edna is hysterical, of course. I hold out my hands upward as if to plead ignorance and then pull Mrs. Bagsley from the pot, meanwhile, my Nails Ale is now a bit too warm for my liking. I feel bad for what I've done, of course, but I'm not going to wreck my soup, either. The kids will be home soon, and now this dog needs to be boned. I dump what's left of the beer into the pot and prep the final steps for the soup.

Easy peasy. Strain and retain the broth, then strip the meat from the bones using a fork. I decide to make dumplings to go along with what's going to end up a rather tender, meaty soup.

Dumplings are dead easy, yet give the impression of having wielded a good amount of culinary skill. Just lower a spoonful into your soup or broth and, after a moment, give a gentle shake and let each dumpling slide off. I made these using prepared couscous, warm butter, eggs, and dill—there's something about Mrs. Bagsley and dill weed that now suddenly seem to go together so well—but you can use what you like. Just separate the eggs first. Then, cream the yolks into the butter, and stir into the couscous and dill until blended evenly. Carefully fold in the egg whites with a wooden spoon, and you're set to go: Dumplings away.

Edna wails into that tattered skirt atop her front steps as I round the corner of her house. Mrs. Bagsley is gone. Gone. Doggie mommies know these things. Of course I'll help you make a LOST DOG sign, I tell her. I take a seat at her side and pass along a fresh bowl of soup with vegetables and dumplings. She trembles and sobs, spoons a bite into her mouth, nods, and thanks me.

You're Soaking in It

Diego always napped on the floor of our living room when Dad went back to work after lunch. And while he napped, for a part of every afternoon, it was me, and not a six-month-old Doberman pinscher puppy, who got to play the part of Mom's best friend.

Together Mom and I shared our little secret of what she called 'Sin and Sacrilege.' Afternoon Soap Operas. She would lay on a love seat and sip a clear drink, ice cubes and happy lemon slices bobbing inside, while I sprawled out on my back atop the blue shag carpeting, near a glass-topped coffee table, and kicked my feet up over my head. I watched, mostly upside down and from between my legs, impossibly beautiful people murmur troubled thoughts, and second-guess the motives of other impossibly beautiful people. All cast within a blurry TV setting, and broadcast through the beige camera filters of some always-warm California.

Beams of afternoon sunlight angled through slats of Mom's wooden window blinds and pierced the clear drink that tinkled in her hand, the rim of her glass smudged a bright coral lipstick-red. Diego slept. I'd lay and wait for Madge, the manicurist and hero of the Palmolive dish soap commercials, to tell a fraught housewife with battered and chapped hands, You're soaking in it. This was a line Mom and I would say together over and over again every day. Sometimes I'd spring to my feet. We'd laugh and laugh.

What? Madge's client would say, aghast, and snatch her hand away. Madge would then calmly press the poor woman's fingertips back down into an ashtray filled with the green syrupy liquid, and Mom and I would call out again that the woman was, in fact, soaking in it.

Once in a while the phone rang. Mom would close her eyes and shake her head for me to ignore it.

I was a good listener.

Diego had been my brother Michael's puppy. He showed up one afternoon with a soft mouth, sharp pointy ears, and size-twelve puppy paws. We got him after Michael died in a motorcycle crash.

Michael had been living in a house with his best friend, Darla, when he died, and I'd almost forgotten he bought a puppy after he got back from the war in Vietnam. I was nine years old and ached for a dog. Literally ached. Any dog. And my insides twisted alternately between delight and grief, and guilt and glee, to learn of an orphaned puppy— *my brother's puppy*—in need of a home. I felt so awful for feeling so happy.

Michael was thirteen years older than I was. He was always this big person to me—thick sideburns, muscular arms, tattoos, cigarettes, and a Harley-Davidson motorcycle— with little more than a detached biological connection to the rest of us still living at home. It was like he belonged to a different family or was the head of his own. And with Michael instantly no longer with us, I all of a sudden found myself struggling to remember anything about him. So part of me hoped that having Diego around would help me hang on to what memories of Michael I did have. Remember him a little better.

The way it worked out, people called me Michael half the time anyway, so it got to where he was pretty hard to forget. I think it was because people said I was a dead-ringer for my brother, but getting called Michael seemed to happen more once we got Diego.

Michael used to talk about Darla a lot. They were always running around with each other. They went to the breeder's together, too. Darla told us that she was the one who actually named the puppy Diego. And that she was there when Michael picked him out of a black-and-tan squall of snoozing, nursing, squeaking puppies. And now with Michael gone, she wanted to keep Diego. She was so attached.

Mom was attached, too. To Michael, not Diego. I heard her talking to Darla on the phone after Michael died. Michael's car, Darla could keep. But not the dog. A living, breathing bond to her oldest boy she lost in an ugly motorcycle crash weeks after he returned safe and sound from the war. No, Mom would be keeping the dog.

The next day, or maybe the day after, here was Diego. Darla sat cross-legged on the floor of our back porch and wept. She sniffed and wiped her eyes. We all watched. She smeared dark eyeliner across the top of a cheek. The edges of her tanned kneecaps poked through frayed rips in her jeans. She was wearing one of Michael's shirts. She pulled strands of straight sandy brown hair from her face and spoke. She had the darkest eyes. Black like Diego's shiny coat.

Michael lay on his side at the breeder's, she said, near the puppies, for nearly an hour. Just kept staring and smiling and shaking his head. He wanted them all, I could tell, she said.

Then this one puppy came over to Michael, she said, and licked his hand. Michael looked up at me, eyes all hopeless. I teared up, she said. It was so sweet.

That's the puppy we took home, she said. That was Diego. Diego the Doberman. She raised her eyes and thumped Diego's rib cage and wiped her nose and smeared more makeup.

Darla handed me the leash. I was crying too. I felt bad for her. She asked if she could come visit sometime.

She kept staring at me. Those dark eyes so black. It was intense, and I didn't know what to say, really, but finally just settled on *Okay*. She hugged me long, smoothed back my bangs, and looked at me hard. She pressed her forehead into mine. I felt her tremble.

James, she whispered. You . . . She stood slowly and leaned down and kissed my forehead. Her face was really warm. You take . . . care, she said. She backed away with another penetrating look. Diego pulled at the leash. He was so strong. I had to plant my feet to hold him back. We all watched her walk away. Diego whimpered and pulled again. She got into Michael's car. I could smell her tears on my cheek as she drove off.

Every morning after we got Diego, Dad went in to work, I rode off on my Schwinn to baseball practice, and Mom walked Diego to the park for his daily obedience training. She applied make-up and bright-red lipstick, put on a colorful summer dress, and pulled on a broad-brimmed straw hat and a big pair of dark sunglasses. Sometimes I'd see her disappear around a row of 'rag trees' on the mossy lawn across the street. Rag trees were these squat things with heavy and twisted trunks like an old elephant. They held a certain creepy power over me, probably because they reminded me of the dense grove of trees at the graveyard where Michael was buried.

Mom explained the importance of being able to 'turn' a dog. That is, when a dog tears off in a dead run away from you, say for a squirrel, you can call the dog back. This is important for the animal's safety, she said. What if a car came?

Dad agreed. He always said that he would never tolerate an unruly dog. In fact, he would have been happy to let Darla keep Diego. The dog's probably already too old to properly train anyway, he said.

So, there was that. But I think mostly Dad wanted to let Darla keep Diego because having Diego around just reminded him that Michael wasn't.

Dad always came home for lunch. Lunch and a quick nap, that is. Sometimes Mom napped with him. During the meal, Dad talked about the day's happenings down at the family hardware store, and Mom talked about her morning successes and failures at training Diego: Sit. Stay. Come.

Dad never seemed very interested, but he did notice how Mom clung to that dog. Mom's voice would catch as she talked about Diego's progress. Dad would shrug, and it was as though every new thing Mom tried to teach Diego pushed my parents farther apart.

Diego wasn't a very speedy learner. Mom could get him to *sit* one day, and *stay*, only to find the need to start all over again the next. It was as if a sprint through the park and a good night's doggie sleep erased it all. Did it erase all of Michael, too?

One morning, while I finished breakfast in the kitchen, Mom and Dad started shouting at each other in the next room. I was watching an episode of *Laurel and Hardy* on the tiny black-and-white screen of the kitchen TV when I heard the yelling start.

I was confused. Our house was always pretty calm and quiet, and my parents never argued much less fought. Never the explosive uproar like the next-door neighbors, the ones always with the dark stains under their arms, with their daily outbursts of cussing and screaming and swearing. No, Mom and Dad weren't like that, not at all, but they seemed to have more moments like this one once we got Diego. Him being a slow learner didn't help.

I peeked around the corner. I knew well enough not to interrupt my mom and dad, but I had to walk through the part of the house that they were fighting in to grab my baseball stuff. But doing so seemed as scary and unwise as running out into traffic. I mean, who would do such a thing, right? Yet, I knew Coach would really lay into me and make me run laps after practice if I was late . . . So I peered around the corner again.

Just watch him! Mom cried. Just once! Just watch what Diego can *do*, Ronald, she shrieked. *Please*.

Honey, Dad said, and sighed deeply. Show me tonight. I'm begging you . . . I'm already late! he said.

That was Dad's name, Ronald. He always seemed like a different person when Mom called him that.

He twisted from her grasp and left in a huff at the very last minute before I walked through the living room. Mom's eyes were small and wet.

I needed to grab my stuff, but felt I had to rescue her from this mood too. Some sort of distraction. So, I decided to sing along with an ad on the TV. But Mom didn't turn her head. If only it had been Madge! Mom squatted down beside Diego and whispered something into his ear, over and again, as she stared at Dad's truck pulling away. Off to work.

It was always 'off to work' with Dad. But this was different. Something bigger was going on here. I stepped closer. She trembled, and her breath chuffed out short and quiet. And sweet, like syrup. He doesn't care, Mom sobbed, into Diego's pointy ear. He doesn't.

Dad's truck stretched around the corner and disappeared behind the twisted rag trees.

I'd never seen Mom like this. My stomach was a tangle of weeds.

He does care, I said, not really knowing if Dad did or not, then dutifully sang along with the theme song of the morning Soap *Love of Life*, which resumed on the TV set in the room behind us.

Mom sat on the floor, silent and still. So still. A fly could have landed on her nose. Even the puppy, sitting and staying for once, was conspiratorially quiet and unmoving.

I turned and took a step into the TV room and there was Madge! Soothing the distraught. The power of a miracle flowed through me. Madge! I whipped around in Mom's direction and called out, delighted, You're soaking in it, Mom! and turned back to the TV set.

But Mom didn't laugh. She didn't even react. She'd gotten up off the floor and was standing in the kitchen with her back to me. The hem of her light dress brushed the curve of her calves. Her shoulders shook. Ice clattered into a glass. The TV screen dimmed. Mom poured from a bottle, and Madge faded from view.

Coach kept me after practice to run laps that day, and I returned home pretty late for lunch, certain I was really gonna get it. Especially considering Mom and Dad's fight that morning. I hesitated in the back yard near the voluminous peonies for a moment, ever fascinated by the blur of sugar ants that writhed brown and black across the plants' slick and enormous buds. Then I stepped into the house to face my parents, to take my medicine.

The screen door hadn't even slapped shut behind me before I could tell that something bad had just happened. Something more than me being late for lunch.

No more, Dad was saying. I . . . can't do this . . . Again.

I stood in the kitchen and stared down at the holes in my socks. My thoughts gurgled with Listerine and became a tangle of marketing jingles. Gradually, I became aware that the *something* was still happening. Something that no Quicker-picker-upper, or porcelain tub filled with a soothing Calgon bath could take anyone away from, even for a little while.

I thought of the peonies outside, buds pulsating like dark throbbing fists.

Well, I certainly don't see what difference it makes! Mom said. Why, no difference at all, she cried, her voice all breathy. You stop and have one on your way home from work, now, don't you, Ronald? You and the fellas!

That is *not* the same, Dad said. Not the same as *this*. And it's not every day! He scoffed and paused. I shouldn't have to put up with this, Elaine, he said, and walked away.

How is it not the same? Mom said. Her sharp shoes clacked anxiously behind him, *clack clack clack*.

All that's different is that you're down at the bar with your buddies and I am here, she said. Alone, *clack*. Her voice caught. With . . . Diego. She breathed loudly and looked around. I felt the palms of her hands press to her face.

And of course James . . . she said, and cleared her throat. I raised my head in the other room, where I pretended not to hear any of this.

Dad drifted down the hall. His voice faded away. Mom's clacking shoes stopped all at once. Dad must have spun back at her, because his voice seemed close and clear. Just don't you make me mark the bottles again! he barked.

Darla dropped by for a visit right about the yawning part of summer, when the oak shadows start to stretch across neighborhood lawns. I didn't really get to see her. Would have been nice, though. I liked Darla. But I was on my way back from the creek when she pulled away in Michael's car. She had black smears on the tops of her cheeks again. She kinda looked my way, but I think she was too busy driving to really see me.

Mom stood in the driveway, arms folded across her yellow dress. She looked like someone just punched her in the stomach. I walked up to her. I didn't say anything. The golden air all around us buzzed with cicadas.

After a while, I asked if Michael's girlfriend came to visit Diego.

Mom's jaw swung open. She turned to me and stroked my hair. She spoke quietly. Darla says she's doing okay, Mom said. But that . . . it will probably be a very long time . . . before she ever . . . gets married.

Mom's voice shook, and she looked away and pressed the back of a hand to her mouth. I kept looking down the street where Darla disappeared, remembering her smell when she drove away on the day she brought Diego.

The next day, Diego bolted into the street as I got home from practice. I heard a car coming around the corner. Mom shrieked and shrieked his name, but Diego kept running and her cries deflated. She couldn't turn her dog. I felt my stomach drop, and I got itchy all over.

The car zeroed in on Diego. I threw down my bike and sprinted to the street after him, hollering Diego! Diego! and Mom wailed, Michael! No!

But Diego streaked ahead. I had to save him. I ran faster and faster. I heard Mom's voice one last time before I flung myself between a speeding station wagon and Michael's dog.

I landed on the other side of the street, thudded up against the twisted trunk of one of those burly rag trees on that mossy lawn. My side hurt. I slowly opened my eyes. The graveyard! I was horrified. Was I dead? What about Diego?

Then I heard Mom. She wobbled above me, moaning and rocking on her knees and screaming my name just inches from my face. Her forehead was blotchy red and shuddered with huge beads of sweat. Diego was nowhere to be seen. Surely, he'd been flattened.

The neighbor with the dark heavy armpits told us that the driver managed to zigzag in such a way as to miss us both. Like a miracle, he said. He shook his head. His voice rattled in the back of his throat like he'd just seen Jesus. A miracle, he repeated.

The neighborhood kids, my supposed friends, the ones who saw that car's unholy maneuver, and Diego bound out of the way, avoided me for a while after that. Like they were afraid.

Dad talked to me that night. Said he didn't believe in miracles. Not the way our neighbor with the dark armpits did. He told me that the driver just had to figure out which way I was going to throw myself so as to swerve around. And Diego? Not listening to Mom, Diego effortlessly sprang to safety, watched the car whiz by, and barked himself around and around in circles after it passed.

I stayed home from practice the next day because my ribs hurt so much. Dad walked in at lunchtime. Mom walked toward the living room from the kitchen, but caught herself with a wobbling stop on the countertop. Dad seized up mid-stride. He turned and walked away without a word. Diego raised up from his nap in the middle of the floor and followed Dad. He seemed distant and small, his face the same shape as when he told me that miracles weren't real. He walked to the basement door and clumped, forever, down the steps. It was like some slow march of dread with the dog behind him all the way down there until I heard him groan and the couch springs squeak.

Mom leaned against the entry to the living room. Her face hung, slack and flushed, and her eyes sagged. I lay atop the blue shag next to the glass coffee table, peering at the TV screen through the peaks of my knees, praying for Madge. Mom's eyes scanned the shelves, then a side table, and slid across the room, where the orbit of her swimming gaze met mine. Madge couldn't save us from this.

I twitched my head at the glass tabletop. Mom nodded and reached for her clear tumbler, basking in a fold of afternoon sun. She turned the glass in her hand and eyed the tired lipstick stains that clouded the rim, and the morning's happy lemon slices, dried and dimmer now, stuck to the bottom.

Then It Would Be Raining

I am not a cutter, I just happen to cut myself a lot. It's not a personal issue, I don't think. What I need, is to be more mindful. More mindful in the kitchen. But it's been hard now, with Mitch like this. Plus, I have lots of distractions going on in my head. A busy place, the insides of my head. I also have a lot of dull knives. Dull kitchen knives are dangerous. Which reminds me . . . I should sharpen those knives. And get cutting. Vegetables . . . Kids will be home soon. Also, I need a band-aid.

The fresh layer of snow in the yard below our bedroom window bounces a silver moonlight blue. Silent and powerful. Tainted only by the McCallans' Christmas display across the street. Red, blue, green, the house announces, this is the outline of our windows, blink, blink. Red, blue, green, this is the perimeter of our front door, it proclaims, blink, blink. Red, blue, green.

Christmas lights in March.

Mitch asleep on the bed behind me breathes hard. Hard-*er*. Something going on in his head, too. Bad things, all of a sudden, all again. Screaming nightmares, every night now since last fall. Dreams I can't sleep through and he can't wake from in a place I could never, ever enter. Can't tell me about them, he says. It's very dark where he sleeps.

During the day, he drifts away.

185

Away from me, away.
Away from us.
Away, I fear, to stay.

I work at a place called Puente. Means 'bridge' in Spanish. It's an organization dedicated to helping individuals with cognitive disabilities live more independently. Connect with and contribute to their community. Often these people—we call them clients—have physical impairments too. I used to work the floor more than I do now, hands-on with our crew to aid clients in walking or tasks requiring more manual dexterity. Using scissors, peeling vegetables, lacing shoes. Things like that. It's challenging work. Some clients eventually catch on. Most don't.

But now I wear a skirt and heels and help run the place, make larger decisions for the greater good of the greater group. I still walk the floors, but mostly my work is on computers and telephones explaining to someone about a great opportunity to hire one of our clients for their menial labor deficits, and how much it won't cost them.

Clients. Our name for our damaged.

I didn't really know Mitch very well when we got married. Some couples come and go on and off for years until they're finally sick enough of each other to get married. Not Mitch and me. Got married while we still burned for each other. Less than a year after we met at a bus stop in Madison.

It was April and snowing these large sugar-cookie snowflakes. He looked at me looking up University Avenue, pulling at my bangs and gasping into a torrent of snow and said, "Mornin—nice day, eh?" He winked, the snow swirling like stars all around his black curls, and I said, "I spose though I sure wish it'd warm up justa bit."

"Yes," he said, slowly, unloading a devastating smile. "Then it would be raining."

Today Mitch totes yet more boxes from our bedroom closet. "I had to forge your signature today," I say, as he elbows by, clutching a heavy cardboard cube to his chest.

"Fine," he says, not looking back. "You sign my name better than I do anyway, Bren." He laughs, and opens the door to the cellar.

Sounds like something Mitch would normally say. And for a moment, I think it's him again. That he's back. Until he resurfaces to cower out of my way and begin taking down shirts from hangers, one at a time, and fold them up, destined for another box to be stored in the root cellar. It's taken me a while to figure it out, but I just now realized that he's moving down there, the root cellar.

The cuts, the old ones, now are mostly all healed. Enough of them run up and down my arms that I started reading about cutters. The psychology of cutting one's own flesh. There's a lot of counter-intuitive logic to cutters that makes perfectly good sense. Mostly boils down to matters of personal control, a coping mechanism. Some self-medicate with booze, others with knives.

But like I said, I am not a cutter.

I don't know what Mitch does during the day anymore. Climbs up from the root cellar every morning, eyes all glazed and crusty, scratches at himself, and leaves the house. No idea where he goes, what he does. I thought he liked his new career, software. He just decided one day he was done being a lawyer and went back to something he "used to poke at semi-legally." So, he bought some computer books and fiddled with his resume and got a job writing code for a software company. I thought he was happy, but why all the nightmares and screaming in his sleep? Why all these fresh cuts on my flesh?

This has been going on for weeks and weeks now. People giving me odd looks because I am starting to look desperate. Me, the one without the personal problem. No, I got no problem, I'm just married to one, I want to say. I want to write it down on index cards and hand them out to whoever looks at me like that. But the pen's over an arm's length away and that stupid effort to reach out for it seems a lot of work for me now. Just raising my eyelids can be too much.

What time is it?

"Where's the car?" I ask Mitch this morning. He came home sometime after I fell asleep reading to Carlie, and now the car's nowhere in sight.

"Here," he says, extending the keys, hunched over a laptop on the kitchen counter. Hi-def screen filled with code and gobbledegook. Meaningless to me, but rather upsetting to him, apparently. I don't think he's been to bed in days.

"Thanks. So, where's the car?"

"Fuck," he says to the computer. "Outside," he says to me.

"*Where* outside?"

"In the street, Bren," he says. He looks through and beyond me like I'm smoke. "The car's parked outside, Bren," he sighs. He blinks, eyes dried up. "Outside in the street."

Jen came over. Mitch's sister, from Boston. Boston, now, anyways. She's a Sconnie, too, like Mitch. I asked her to come. Jen's an empath—the real deal. Gets readings from a photo, a voice over the phone, watching a crowd in a bar, seeing a guy round the corner a block up the street. The chemistry of a person's mental and emotional state emits an odor she can detect and interpret, easily. The way some read sheet music, she says. She sees dreams, the spills of broken love, shapeless, through brick walls.

We embraced. I didn't have to say anything. She looked around the house as Mitch looked right through her on his way out. Jen nothing more than a lamp or a vase that'd always just been there like the trim around the windows. Maybe he knew she was coming the way she knew something was very wrong before she even got here. Sometimes I wonder if he's more like her than he lets on.

"Panic," Jen said, watching him walk and twitch and look through us. "In a profound panic."

She didn't seem so surprised. She followed him down to the cellar and I could hear them talking a while. His voice rumbled low, then rose right as he was about to laugh, always with this new, otherly exuberance. She never shared in the laughter though, not that I could hear.

I am not the sort of person who throws things. I want to be—I do. I want to smash the fine china on the kitchen floor and drink bourbon straight from a bottle for days plunked into a corner while I pull shards from the bottoms of my bare feet. Pull them from my feet while drinking and listening to Mitch scream his head off in the cellar, where he lives now, down there. While I pluck, shard by shard, and

189

will my way into his sleep to slice up whatever it is tearing him apart down there.

But I'm not the sort of person who throws things.

Jen is going to stay on a few days, she says. I look across the room at her, then at Mitch, leaning up against the wall, wearing that old, torn-up Badgers sweatshirt, pointer finger two knuckles up his nose. He removes it and starts to say something. Then his words stray, and he stops speaking and puts his finger back up his nose. Jen, at his side, doesn't react.

Apparently we're going to a ski resort this coming weekend.

I am drowning in dirt, dirt that drips. Drips on my face from a sky plowed up mud by a wedge of geese tearing the overhead terrain, dripping on me, a frog in a pot of water slowly brought to a boil, unwittingly dying in its own bath. Drowning in dry dirt inside droplets of raining mud.

We made dinner tonight, me and Jen. Managed not to cut myself. Haven't since she got here. Set a place for Mitch, hoping he'd come up from the root cellar. For once. I pulled the plates from the cupboard, noisily but carefully, passing them one at a time to Jen. I have a memory of plates with room to breathe in there, of coffee cups unafraid of being sent over the edge.

Neighbors' silverware in the drawer at my waist. Del, Diane, Will, Mags. Someone else, too. Don't recall now, but Mom always said ya know ya live in a good neighborhood when half the silverware in there is someone else's. Some of mine is out there, too. In others' drawers. Except for the knives. Those stay right where they belong.

Mitch's plate kept moving, without comment, around the table as Jen and I ate and the kids brawled and cried through dinner. First it was at his normal place, then the other side of the table as we cleared dinner, then at the breakfast counter by the sink in the island. Finally, when Mitch kept not coming, I put his plate back, closed up and away, back behind cupboard doors. Up and away, back in the dark.

Jen touched my shoulder.

I walked down into the root cellar yesterday while Mitch was out doing whatever. Just to see. Exact opposite of what I expected. Figured it'd be all squalor, him sleeping down there like in some storage cell on the edge of town, a slender varmint woven into a warren of piled heaps pushed aside just wide enough for him to traipse through and lie down in.

But it's all in order. Cleaner than when we moved in, even. The stone walls plucked clean of cobwebs, ceiling joists and support beams wiped down and dusted. Floor's been swept. Everything he took from our closet and boxed now stacked neatly, each piece of clothing hung smartly. There's a set of drawers arranged from shoe boxes slipped inside an upright plastic bin. A drawer slides out deftly, where socks are folded with care, not balled up or pushed inside in wads. Towers of books, rising up like in-progress games of Jenga, straddle each end of an old sofa I'd forgotten about. Must be where he sleeps, sort of. Even the porcelain sink in the half-bath reflects a blinding white, and the chrome towel rack gleams.

I stepped into the bath, leaned over the sink for a moment, and looked up at the limestone wall above the faucet where my reflection should have looked back at me. There was just emptiness of exposed stone. I looked down at my fingers resting on the edge of the sink, before that emptiness could pull me in.

This morning Mitch sits opposite me in the breakfast-express room at the hotel near the ski resort, wearing a dingy old night-shirt sporting smeared grease. His bony face twitches, slate-gray eyes sunken like two echoes. His eyes blink rapidly, one at a time. And if he's shaved, it was days ago, the one side of his face.

Jen's doing laps down in the tepid pool. Her word. Said she'd eat an egg later.

In front of a faux fireplace, Mitch's eyes are locked on some local morning newsy program, hosted by perky homecoming royalty from about ten years ago. A local chef introduces the hosts to shrimp and grits. Everyone knows who he is. Royalty smiling, tanned in March, talking loudly—nearly shrieking—clichés, scripted prompts. Eager to please their adoring studio audience. They laugh so easily for their springy star, Courtenay. No lines for great-looking-demure-homecoming king next to her. He hands Courtenay the occasional utensil or measuring cup, widening his eyes for the camera. I think I'm meant to swoon. Name of the show is *Good Courtenay Morning*. And Mitch is gobbling it up.

Shrimp and grits. The hosts rave, find the idea fascinating and amazing. As if their discovery was everyone else's. And *Good Courtenay Morning*? There is nothing about this program that does not scream to Mitch *Please hate me* more than anything else I could think of. Normally, the name alone would make Mitch rant about it off and on again for days.

A family clambers around the table beside ours, eyes all wide for what's on the TV, the fresh snow, the staged fireplace. Our kids fall silent as an impossible number of children pull chairs around the table. Already I can tell all these kids combined will create less mess and make less noise than any one of ours. The coiffed father, seated in plaid L.L. Bean loungewear, straightens himself to answer a daughter.

"Well," he says, loud enough for everyone's attention, "I suppose Santa *could* come to the Ski Chalet today . . . But it's *March*, sweetie."

He gives her a sympathetic smile, reaches to cup her cheek.

A three- or four-year-old girl with protuberant brown eyes and neatly mussed black hair looks up from the Yoplait she's carefully peeled the aluminum foil lid from. She places the lid atop the saucer before her, yogurt-side up at twelve o'clock, next to a glass of juice, unspilled. She unfolds a napkin and flattens it on her lap.

"Aww," she pouts, raising a spoon.

"Santa?" Mitch snorts. "*Santa*? Santa's *busy*, sweetheart! Saw him just last night, pan-handling on the sidewalk down in front of the bowling alley. Said he—"

"Mitch!" I protest, but know that I can't stop him.

"—Said he's fallen on hard times!"

I can't stop him.

"Beggin for hand-outs, Santa suit all soiled." He shakes his head, one eye twitching, then the other. "Jesus . . . Broken fingernails black and poking through these useless gloves, playing a guitar and harmonica and—" he pauses for a minute breath, then his focus lands on something about ninety miles beyond the horizon, "—singin these old Jim Morrison songs . . . you know . . . the *poems*. God," Mitch says, voice breaking, as though he actually witnessed all this, "the guy utterly . . . *reeked*."

Before anyone can react, Mitch leaps to his feet and points urgently down an imaginary roadway.

A couple of L.L. Bean child models turn their heads tentatively, in the direction he's pointing.

"Down there," he cries, looking at them, jabbing a finger at the air. "Down there! Prolly asleep ... and brandy-sodden ... bummin smokes ... down *there* ... right *now!*"

We are cruising aboard an airplane at forty thousand feet, speeding across the continent when someone kicks out the evac door over the wing. A silent roar sucks out the entire room with a deafening force that nearly pulls the ribbons of fake flames in the fireplace out into the cold along with it.

Confused tears surge in the girl's bulbous eyes. She is about to scream. Or giggle wildly. Hard to know with some kids. In normal times, ours would have squealed with delight. Her father opens his mouth, smug grin shattered, like he's suddenly stepped, barefoot, into a pile of something warm and soft. And Courtenay's spilled grits on her tits.

Breakfast is over.

Delphine, a fitness consultant, slinks across the street to our yard, skin-tight everything. Even her new plastic-surgered face looks crazy tight, facial dermis stretched completely to the epi.

Jen ties a shoe a few feet away, about to leave for a run. She looks up from her crouch.

"Something's wrong," she murmurs, straightening up. She pauses for a brief whiff to confirm. "Yep. Yer neighbor's got some *baaaad* news, Bren."

She looks at me, says she, too, has got something to tell me ... later. She flashes a significant nod and disappears in a poof, annoyingly lithe.

Del talks a while and finally I hear myself saying, "Well, what can I say, ya know? Mothers die. Mine died when she found out I wasn't getting married just because I got knocked up like her. She was giddy, me all thin and gettin married not pregnant, Del, and she musta then just let herself stop fightin whatever ailed her, cuz she woke up dead the very next mornin. I'm sorry, Del. Mothers die. They just do."

I fold my arms and look at Del, then down the lane Jen disappeared from, my arms suddenly heavy, the one atop the other, dreading what she's got for me.

Jen went back to Boston the next day. Told me about Mitch's childhood while we stopped for a drink on the way to the airport. About all the abuse. Low-lights Mitch spared me, years of it. Like all the photos, and the man who made Mitch pose for them, year after year, summer after summer. About his prayers for a never-spring, and an always-rain.

I tried off and on again to get Mitch to a doctor, to consult professional help. Always got a calm, Heisman stiff-arm in refusal. Of course he thinks he's fine, always looks at me like I'm the crazy one as he shrinks and coils away.

Then yesterday he one-upped me, and had an accident, somewhere. I couldn't get it outta him where. But he fell down and smashed his ribs. Six ribs, front and back, all staved in up and down the left side. ER visit became a two-day hospital stay that may turn into three or even four. I went to work the middle of Day Two, today, thinking I'd try to get caught up on what's piled up, distract me from myself for a while. Mitch needed rest . . . blood in his urine.

A nurse called as I drove, mentioned how dehydrated Mitch was.

"Needs electrolytes," she said.

"Okay," I said.

"Yes. He must get dehydrated often . . . Just have him drink some Gatorade when that happens next time," she said, all cheery. "That's where you get electrolytes."

"Gatorade," I said. I think she could hear me frowning, so she spoke again before I could.

"Yes. Gatorade is for replenishing essential electrolytes and lost fluids—"

"From Gatorade," I managed to say. Sounded like she was reading this to me. "Can't I just *feed him things* that *contain* electrolytes?" I said. "I mean— Yer serious about the Gatorade? Have ya ever drank it," I asked. "It's disgusting. And fulla sugar. I mean— Yer a nurse . . . ya want him to get *better*, right?"

I could hear her blank stare over the phone, her nurse fingers fluttering over a computer keyboard. Then she re-read to me what she said about the Gatorade.

"Yeah, I get it," I said, and hung up and parked at Puente. Gatorade.

Almost as soon as I walked into Puente today, one of our clients, a guy named Nathaniel—we happen to call him Prana—collapsed right in front of me. His knee caved and contorted at a horrible, berserk angle beneath the full mass of his body. I was still thinking about Mitch. No pierced organs . . . but should I have stayed at the hospital? Looked like he could sleep for a week, like those Russians living by that one uranium mine, sleeping five, six days on end. Hard to know now, especially with Mitch. Mitchell. Mitchell and his night- and daymares, the way he moved from our bedroom into the basement, one box of clothes at a time, and the way he talks about some homeless guy living down in our cellar. Hairy hands, Mitch says, hairy hands like mine, he says, turning his hands over for you to see. Hirsute, he'll tell nearly anyone who'll listen.

I'm pretty sure he's worn the same pair of pants every day now for over a month.

I watched the collapsing Prana's fall and felt the anger and hate ignite within me again. Hate. The real thing. What this man, this locally respected man, this neighborhood Todd person with a thing for little boys did to Mitch, so many years ago. Years and years, a sickening level of abuse. And what it's done to us now a generation later. And me, the oblivious frog, dying within the boiling storming planet around, slowly boiling to death and not seeing and not knowing.

Small wonder he still loves the cold so. Sub-zero temps the only thing that make him feel safe. Ended each night's prayers with . . . *and a winter without end. Amen.*

Del came back to our yard the next day, needed help making phone calls. I said of course I'd help, then remembered telling her about my mother's glee at me getting married thin and not pregnant. I smiled, and Del pounced.

"You think it's funny?" she snapped, the way bossy women do. "My mom dead and me here with no support network and you all grinnin about it?"

I couldn't speak, couldn't put into words why I was smiling. "No," I said, defensive. "No, Del, no. I—"

"Then *what?*" she hissed.

I shook my head and said I'd be over in a little bit. And it wasn't until later I realized I was smiling because I was just recalling my mom fondly. Mom was lovely, despite how much she drove me nuts. So I smiled. And I also think I kept smiling because in spite of Del I was just relieved to finally have something to smile about.

I managed to cushion Prana's fall, grabbing him from behind by the armpits, then tried to hoist him. Hike him up like a child, off that knee I heard pop like an old man's. But Prana is a round, 250-pound man. Probably eighty, ninety pounds overweight. His body, despite the excruciating pain racing through it, remained flimsy and unwieldy. Like a sagging mattress you need to shove up a set of stairs.

My hands buried in Prana's soggy armpits did take my mind off Mitch for a while, though. I slipped off my heels and called out for help. But first I asked a passer-by, a client guardian, to lend a hand.

"I—I don wanna lawsuit," passer-by guy muttered, backing away from Prana and me. He opened his palms and raised his elbows.

"Just a towel," I said. "Just grab a towel from over there." I nodded at a table behind him. "And bring it over."

"No lawsuit, man," he said, tripping away.

I stared, drenched hands still wedged deep up into Prana's hot and squashy armpits, still attempting to gain some leverage and take more pressure off his blown knee. He continued to shriek. I raised my skirt and thrust a knee into his lower back and managed to lift him slightly. Prana groaned, relieved, his pulse a jackhammer ramming at my fingertips pressed beneath a heavy flesh-fold under his jawline.

"Nathaniel," I said, precise. "We are going to call nine one one. Are you comfortable with that?"

"Prana! Pra-*na*!" he gasped, nodding sweaty and fast.

"I know," I said, quietly, nodding with him, "I know."

I yelled. That got the attendants' attention. I told them to call. They gaped.

"Now!"

They called. No-lawsuit guy vanished.

"It's ok," I said into Prana's ear. The back of his sweaty head pressed against my blouse. "It's ok. They're coming," I soothed, weakly. I lifted from under his arms and pried him up with my other knee, pulling him mostly on top of me. His shrieking subsided and he groaned again. His knee remained pinned and bent at a terrible angle beneath all his weight, already exploded, and I feared a stroke or worse.

Then I was up there. Floating on the ceiling. Drifting in and amid promiscuous furry caterpillars. Weaving, blending, copulating, separating, reconnecting black and gray and brownish cream, pushed together within ceiling-tile gardens, forming patterns. Some of the patterns almost spelled out something. In English, maybe. Sodium, magnesium, chloride, potassium. Electrolytes. Some not. All a melded fuzzy gardeny blur above, Prana and I pressed together in a sweaty bulge below.

Every once in a while, the man I fell in love with starting that snowy April morning on University Avenue looks up at me. A few nights before his fall, he gave me that same look after he first said to me, *Then it would be raining.*

"So, ya headin to class?"

"Yup."

"Me neither." He looked down at his watch, enormous snowflakes still looping around his black curls. He smiled up at me again and said, "I'm thinkin it's noon somewhere. Let's hit the 608 for a tap and study up."

He pointed to a tavern down the block over my shoulder. I stared at him.

"Whatcha workin on today?" he asked.

"Today?" I said, more to myself than to him. "Uh . . . today it's . . . Organic Chem."

"Oh."

"Know anything about it?"

"Does it matter? C'mon, let's go," he said, and reached for my hand.

My Mitch. Took him into my arms and held him as long as I could, pulling him back to me until he fell away again, twisting and dissolving, down into that root cellar with his collective rumblings down there, to scream in his sleep and worship the cold and pray for rain.

The sweating man pressed against me was born Nathaniel Phelps. Some call him Nate. Most just call him Prana because that's all he's been able to say since age nineteen, when he found his brother dead in the woods. His brother severed his femoral artery with a Bowie knife while field dressing a deer he'd shot. He had been alone and bled very deeply and very badly two decades before cellphones were commonplace. Prana came upon him at the end of a red trail of blood pools on fresh snow that turned out not to lead someone's shot deer but rather to his brother. Bled out and starting to freeze solid beneath a fresh dusting of mid-November snow. Nathaniel returned to camp muttering *Prana . . . Pra-na.* His family says he sat out in the cold against a tree that night and refused to eat for days. No one has figured out what the utterance can mean. The bled-out frozen brother's name was Wallace. He was seventeen for a day.

Prana's trauma took place in the woods, Mitch's on the banks of a pristine trout stream in Wisconsin. Mitch walked away, mostly. Prana . . . Not so much. Not yet.

"They're everywhere," Jen said, after telling me about the man who used to take Mitch supposedly fishing down on Noisy Creek.

"Creeks?"

"No."

When Mitch awoke, the doctor who treated him for his ribs sent in a psychiatrist. He wore a white lab coat like any other house doc, so Mitch didn't suspect much. They talked and talked and when he left, he told me Mitch would be following up with him at his practice. Consult for a wicked, ongoing experience with PTSD, he said to me. Dissociative Fugue. Said Mitch wouldn't remember much of this. If anything, he added. Said his brain's running in survival mode. On autopilot.

Dissociation. Of course. I nodded on the outside, but on the inside called myself a blind and stupid bitch for not spotting this sooner. How could I have missed all the signs?

The shrink in white lab coat left, giving me a knowing look as he reached for my hand, then stopped short when he saw the marks on my arm. He looked at me again, hesitated, and wished me well.

Prana cries and cries in my arms, back of his head tucked under my chin. EMS shows up at last, and I'm finally able to walk over to the restroom, where I peel off my drenched blouse and bra and plop them onto the counter by the sink in front of the mirror. There I am, hands slung loosely at my sides, staring back at me, only me, me alone. And my bare breasts coated in a strange man's sweat.

I hear them wheel Prana away. A sense of tidal loss engulfs me. Can't explain it. An emptiness that presses my lungs shut.

But soon enough I'm bent over the sink, staring at my fingertips. Tender goat udders dripping thick threads of tainted milk. All the Prana, all of no-lawsuit guy, all the Todd. All dripping out. Even the Gatorade nurse and the spilled shrimp and grits. All of it all. Drips from the tips of each finger, one finger each for the P, the T, the S, and the D.

My bright new blood congeals on the side of the porcelain basin. The bathrooms here are always chilly, and this has happened before. The sink is cold and so my blood stops. And I breathe into my blood, clotted on the slope of the sink, breathing into it my warmth, and watch the red spirals glow, loosen, and turn to rain.

Sometimes Creek

Our move to Halloween Street was one of necessity, not choice. Following the death of my wife, Sylvia, the home we had rented was sold. The new owners gave us nine months to vacate. And this place, situated on a leafy and wealthy street in the town's eerie historic district, was the only thing available within walking distance of my daughter Claire's school. So I took it, despite the steep rent commensurate with the austere economic laws of *Supply and Desperation*.

An energetic and put-together neighbor tells me I will need somewhere between three and four thousand pieces of candy, treated out one piece per kid, as well as gallons of a stiff grog for parents, to get me through the hours-long Halloween night here on Halloween Street. Based on some simple arithmetic and plot-pointing along a mental timeline, starting with the next paycheck, I have just enough pay periods between now and the end of October to buy a total of 4,000 pieces of candy. Or eight hundred pieces of candy each payday, all totaling in the end approximately six hundred American dollars. Candy. For one happy motherless night for our only child more than two months hence.

It is barely August.

EIGHT WEEKS TO HALLOWEEN. News of us renting the old Demello house has spread, our transience rather well known. In an old neighborhood like this, even the friendly

203

are reluctant to bond with the ephemeral. Brent from up the street makes an effort though, and introduces us as 'the family from that one accident' that's 'holing up in the Demellos' tax shelter.'

Brent is referring to the spectacular car crash in which my wife, and our baby girl growing inside her, scarcely the size of Claire's fist, died. A sister we had yet to tell Claire to get ready for.

I look at Brent. It's hard to feel embarrassed for a stranger, and worse when everyone witnesses your embarrassment, particularly when everyone knows what the stranger means in the first place. I'm still trying to make the house something we can think of as a home while figuring out how to explain to Claire, once and for all, that Sylv isn't coming back. My first-grader shouldn't be made to feel like a drifter. Bad enough her mom is gone for good.

In a matter of days, Claire has sorted out new friendship circles, and broadened existing ones. And she has adapted to hand-language thanks to one child she hadn't known.

Jasmine, the non-verbal girl who lives opposite our house. She's eight, with the height of a twelve-year-old. Cloud of fawny brown hair, bright ashen eyes, she's beautiful. She drapes a blue velvet cape around her shoulders and uses a gnarled tree branch for a magic staff. She's calm and inviting though our speechless hands and confused eyes disappoint, I can tell.

Claire wasted no time connecting. Those luminous and arresting eyes glimmering from the rounded front porch corner of that Queen Anne summoned Claire, who offered little resistance. Together she and Jasmine colored on the sidewalks, dug for worms, chased grasshoppers, and nibbled columbine beneath the warm late-summer sun. Claire paged through stacks of books and narrated her version of the action, dirty wormy fingers pointing at the occasional word as Jasmine nodded along. Then they braided and unknotted each other's hair and shook like dogs and laughed and laughed and dug up more bird worms and fed them to the trout in the small creek that flows somewhere behind the Queen Anne.

All this time I lived in this town, I said to Claire, and I never knew that little river existed.

She giggled and massaged the air in front of her as she spoke: It's only there once in a while. 'Sometimes Creek' comes and goes, she said. Her fingertips drew toward her: Comes. And goes, she said. Her fingertips looped and fell away.

Now Claire and the nonverbal girl routinely disappear into the long-grassed and misty beyond of Sometimes Creek. It's hard to explain how they vanish around the corner of that house. That big old Queen Anne, with the blurry circular porch corners. Jasmine hoists her staff up high, unfurls her cape, and they clasp hands and swing around a kudzu lattice into a knee-deep mist.

Once upon a time there was a messy little girl…

Jasmine's mother, Rain, shows relief at the sight of Claire bounding across the street to her daughter. She and I chat. She's also a single parent now. Doesn't offer much, just that Geoff *had to go*. She's tall with a mossy green countenance, and soft honey skin that will seem slightly tanned even in December. Rain wears solid, ankle-length cotton dresses and moves like an adult version of her daughter. A plume of clove and anise wafts from her aura.

There's no pretense about Rain, and her eyes don't slide away as she speaks to you or as you speak to her. A stray hair that sprouts from the space between her eyebrows reminds me of something. Something Sylv would pluck, probably, but Rain doesn't seem to mind. Behind her, a misty distortion rises where the edge of her side of the street begins, and all I detect is lush.

She's content, she says, to care for her little girl, and her home, just like me. She appears to like the fact that Claire dresses herself, has knotty hair that Jasmine needs to pull apart and straighten out every morning, and usually has clumps of berry jam or smears of maple syrup all over her skirt.

I return the gratitude, and comment on how well Jasmine functions despite her disability.

Rain's eyebrows shoot up. Disability? she says. A quick pit rots in my stomach.

I was embarrassed for Brent, but Rain, in this moment, is not embarrassed for me. But I detect she senses that I'm aware of a gaffe.

Jasmine is *non-verbal*, Rain says, and smiles the way one would when clarifying the color of their eyes. *Hazel, not brown.* We watch Jasmine explain something patiently to Claire with her hands.

Rain places a hand on a hip and tilts her neck. Her lips curl into a wry smile. She knows she's got me. Does my daughter look disabled to you?

I smile and shake my head, Of course not.

After a while, Rain asks so what's my story.

It's a good question. But our talk of Jasmine makes me think about Claire, who already speaks with concurrent hands and mouth. I wonder if there's ever a miscommunication, or a language overlap with her hands. If the speech of her hands is always true to the language of her mouth. A language tangle. Collision of words, or a disagreement in conveyance. Doesn't matter. She's convinced she's got it right.

Mostly I wonder if her signing cuts like her voicing. Like earlier today, when she asked, Will I remember her?

So many dewy morning moments like this, her sleepy voice, messy hair, broken toenails, all pressed against me beneath the covers, warm honey breath asking, asking, asking, asking.

Any memory at all?

I shudder and lift my eyes to Rain, who waits to hear so what's my story. I exhale only once and my story is done.

She winces audibly, and clutches me, on my front lawn, beneath the buzz of summer leaves. She smells like grassy sunshine and roasting fennel. The warmth of her face presses into mine. She feels me shake. I close my eyes. She doesn't let go.

The smells of early fall creep into our house. Summer's last dust scales the girls' shins while their tireless hands laugh and gab on this side of the street and that. Usually that side of the street. I ask Claire why Jasmine doesn't come over more often.

Hers is the *best* place, Claire says. She glances around.

After more than a month, I still call the Demello tax shelter our *house*. Not our *home*, despite how homey I try to make this empty place feel. Empty, yet so full of what Sylv would say, the little things she'd do to make all this less like something of my own doing. Tip her long neck to a side, look at me with those amused black eyes, twitch her crooked smile, and save me from myself.

Sylv never knew this house. So, I can't call what I now detect a 'lingering.' Yet her absence perseveres, and persists. A pressure that inflates every room. Radiates in nooks, corners, and questions—Mom? Mom?—new, known, unknown, and unborn.

Present events fold into the past so quickly. Everything, even that which lies well ahead of me, becomes consumed by the proactive machinery of retrospective, grinding and dissolving and blowing away. A rear-view mirror always blocking my view of what approaches, obstructing my path. The echoes and reflections of my immediate past—Dad? Dad? Where's Mom?—are all I can see coming at me.

Today Claire comes buzzing inside while I'm struggling to hang a bookshelf. The physical hanging part is easy. The struggle lies in the placement, plagued with Sylv's in-my-head second-guessing. How she'd organize and position such things as books, pottery, music, little pretties. This location on the living room wall would clearly prove to be the incorrect spot were Sylv around. But it seems good enough to me, for now.

I set down my drill and tell Claire to wash her face. She wipes her mouth and checks the back of her hand.

It's just mustard, she says, looking up. She raises a hand to spell out the word.

Oh?

Yep. Jasmine's always got a just-in-case-wich in her sack.

A just-in-case-wich? I say. What's that?

Claire sighs and rolls her eyes and shakes her head and positions her feet like Sylv.

It's a sandwich! You know . . . for just in case.

Ah, I say, reminded that I should eat something myself.

Yep. Sometimes we split it. Cheese and mustard.

Oooh. Sounds good.

Occasionally, the truth comes out to play. But I can't. Not yet. Some days, though, I think I'm over it. But usually, I'm not. I still have the need to put on a happy mask, file down the sharp edges of the story. Though Claire, less restless, more content now with her discovery of Jasmine and her spell of signing, seems more easily satisfied with my simple explanations. What happened to our other house? What I don't tell her is that our previous home on the other side of this small town, where we lived when Sylv was killed, was demolished shortly after we moved away. What I said earlier about the house getting sold off wasn't exactly true. There was no reason to move other than Sylv's suffocating absence. We had to leave. But the part about the Demellos' place is true: this crazy expensive house was the only thing available near Claire's school.

Real estate developers are now constructing an office building where our home once stood. I told Claire that the new owners wanted to build a place for workers. She shrugged and galloped across the street.

It seems that only now, a full month in this house, have I been able to ponder any of this. Yet I still have no words. How could anyone, really? My wife and unborn daughter a highway traffic statistic, the drunk driver roaming free and still piling into things, racking up a DUI every other year. I have no words for this. How could anyone?

Just candy. A growing stockpile tucked away in the dank basement laundry room of a spendy rental on a wealthy street.

Four weeks out. The Halloween spirit more than stirs. Corporate retailers have been marketing to children for weeks. I add to my candy stockpile every payday. Last time it was Kit-Kats. School has been in full motion for nearly a month, and the autumnal equinox has passed. We've had nights of frost, many species of apples are ripe, and birch trees are shedding their leaves, albeit in an unsettling and premature global-warming sort of way. Too soon dead. An adult elephant, meandering through the same room as me in a different part of my brain, makes a desperate plea for me to just ignore him.

A neighbor pulls up alongside our curb in her new pickup truck while I'm standing outside, arms folded, considering the lifeless leaves.

The neighbor is absurdly beautiful. Her truck revs. The horn beeps. The leaves loop and land, dead, dry, and indifferent.

Hello! she shrieks, and extends a sculpted arm from her new pickup truck. Michaela. Dark curls, clear skin, alive eye-whites.

How *are* you, Cyprian?

Good, thanks. I'm—

Great! I'm so *glad*, she says. And I think she is glad. She smiles gigantically.

We're just back from the pumpkin patch! She points over her shoulder toward the bed of her truck. My line of sight crosses the four glowing eyes of her two girls, staring out at me, the father of the noisy messy child renting the Demello house. The kid who prefers the non-verbal girl to them.

At least forty happy pumpkins swell inside the bed of Michaela's truck. Picked, trimmed, and polished. Gleaming orange, purple, white, and black. Perfectly clean. She's acting pleasant enough, but her jaw dangles, and her lips remain parted, in some form of indictment. I see her eyebrows rumple as she squints around my yard, eyes angling toward my stoop.

Her teeth flash. The Demellos, she says, *really* used to light this place up! Her eyes flicker and drift toward my stoop again.

All I've got that's remotely relevant is my candy. But not now. She's in the middle of a moment with her girls, and they took time out to share, to check on me, to see how I'm doing. Perhaps even Michaela, now with a polite little laugh that could scarcely fill a champagne glass, is capable of seeing beyond her own untouchable beauty to notice that there is clearly something wrong with me. She'd clutch me, too, maybe, were her DNA wired for it.

Gotta keep the Hallo*ween* in Hallo*ween* Street! she says, and lets loose that champagne-glass laugh again. The whites of her eyes light up the inside of the cab. She revs her truck. She doesn't hop out to clutch me. She turns her head to drive away when one of her girls blurts something I don't catch. The girl's head turns in my direction, wide eyes finding mine. Michaela's lips remain parted. She hesitates, nods to her daughter, and offers me a pumpkin.

Go ahead, she says, tossing back curls. The light always catches her hair just right. Take one, she says.

Air crowds into my lungs. I step toward her truck.

Thank you, I say.

Just don't grab it by the stem! she says.

I select one at random and hoist it to my chest. It's heavier and more dense than I expect. The thick stem smells like freshly cut vine. My throat has gone dry. I back away from the truck and nod.

Michaela, she yelps, reminding me yet again, and presses a palm to the tops of her breasts, breathless. Shiny dark curls tumble over the back of her hand. She revs goodbye. I've barely nodded again before her teeth are done glinting and she's pulled away out of sight.

Time exhales, and cascades out of control, off the rails. A lateral waterfall sprawl. October? It's a month that's appeared here, before me, spun like a scarf from a hole in the middle of this Halloween Street air. An air that now quickens with anticipation, and a certain anxiety. Like a prolonged breath held trapped within a lung for an extra second, and then another.

Pumpkins line every porch top, and it's just now occurred to me that not only does every house on this street boast a spacious front porch, each porch has a flat rooftop, and each flat rooftop is now lined with pumpkins. Not jack-o'-lanterns just yet, though it's been cold enough for those.

Jasmine across the street signs something that reminds me that I haven't put away all of the day's shopping, and a couple of new things happen at once. The first is that it looks like I started to put things away, like groceries and yet more Halloween candy, but I became yet again distracted and wandered away from bulk spices and dry goods into some remote brain ether. In this case to observe twirling dying dead leaves. Then a weight presses, deliberately, across the back of my shoulders, into my shoulder blades.

Ghosts only get lost for a little while. Do they stop to ask for directions? Who or what would they ask? And how? Maybe they sign, too. Like Jasmine to Claire. I don't know. But I'm relatively convinced that a motivated ghost will eventually find you, and this pressure upon my back is not entirely new. It's been creeping into me at random since the funeral.

This touch is startling at first, but once settled in, I don't want it to leave. The only thing I dread, in fact, is its departure. The wondering if this time will be the last.

I mention this to a work colleague over lunch. She doesn't look up from her soup when she tells me, calmly, that I am 'a natural draw for those new at being dead.' I nearly drop my sandwich.

So, bulk spices, among other items, still need a home, to be put away. At my replacement house, from which I'm trying to carve a home, I repurpose empty spice jars. New labels for old spice and herb containers. A new, replaced creation of what it will contain, from the old.

The empty jar in my hand will become dried peppermint, and I suppose I do replace, like that one poet said: *Women mourn, men replace.*

But Sylv isn't a thing, and she's not empty. Only thing empty is this jar in my hand. I turn it between my fingers, and wish I could climb inside and twist the lid.

I close my eyes.

Once upon a time, there was a man who didn't want to replace. Who didn't want to move on, didn't want to just get over it.

213

Savory becomes oregano, thyme becomes tarragon, clove becomes coriander, and fennel becomes…

Anise. I open my eyes and look up and out the front window across the street. Warm anise wafts in from Sometimes Creek, where beautiful Rain makes black licorice.

She offered me a piece the other day. I hesitated.

Go ahead, she urged, and smiled secretively. What? You've never had homemade licorice before? She laughed quietly and coiled a length of hair over an ear. C'mon, she cackled, like I was acting silly. She nudged me with the plate. It's even gluten free.

I stare at the jar in my hand and fasten the replacement label *Mint* with a band of clear tape, and it's hard to remember what the peppermint was for. A stir-fry? Claire shrieks from across the street. Maybe she's caught a trout. Or a hairy spider. The inside of this old house throbs with changes Sylv would make. Halloween hype amps up. Maybe the mint was for a stir-fried something-or-other. I don't know. I can't even remember the last time I made rice. Maybe water is freezing on a lake somewhere. And all of the dead leaves on the ground can each individually rise all together, all at once, and reattach to their trees, pulled up from the ground by a resurrecting tree-branch magic. I don't know. I don't. And I can't. Can't remember anything. Like what the mint was for. Can't remember anything at all. Except that Sylv and our baby girl are still dead.

DAY ZERO. HALLOWEEN. Claire bangs around inside the house somewhere, searching out a shoe to work with her costume. This year she's going as a Q-tip. Neighbors have lit their jack-o'-lanterns, one continuous row, house to house to house to house, a thread of gleaming pumpkins, flashing

214

toothy smiles, pulsing out a visual melody. She rummages and I lean over the kitchen sink to eat a leftover something. My tongue is dry and numb, the something chalky and wet.

In the laundry room, the box holding the Halloween candy stash feels suspiciously light. Nearly empty, in fact, but I carry it up the stairs anyway to check the bags inside. They're all empty. Each and every bag.

Not a single Snickers, packet of M&M's, or Kit-Kat bar remains. I swear they were all there a few days ago.

It's Halloween. Month zero, week zero, day zero. *The* day. I'm standing on the front stoop. My lights are lit. A column of hot flames twists inside Claire's jack-o'-lantern. The street is blocked off for pedestrian traffic only. A TV news crew has set up beyond the street barricade, an earnest reporter geared up for her annual *Live from Halloween Street* news segment. Throngs of kids and their excited parents will push through at any minute. There will be so many kids. I can hear the jeer of jack-o'-lanterns atop porches up and down the street, mocking me. So many jack-o'-lanterns. Their flickering voices all sniggering as one.

Michaela and her perfect curls wander by and ask if I'm all set. This time, she spares me the self-introduction. I recall back in August, when she first explained the Halloween Street Rules: Three to four thousand kids; one piece per kid; adult grog for parents; lights out and disappear when candy gone. She helps herself to a glass of mulled wine. She nods at the jack-o'-lantern carved from the pumpkin she gave us. Nice, she says, smiling indulgently. She looks at me, recalling that moment. One I mistook for compassion but now understand was pity.

I cough and notice that her place down the block is all dark.

Outta candy already? I joke, tired, and gesture toward her house.

She seems taken aback. Her hair tosses. Eh? Oh. No, she says, and chuckles that breathy champagne-glass laugh.

She stoops before me slowly to top off her drink, then straightens and leans back, resting an elbow in her free hand. Michaela's still mid-chuckle when she says, We *never* hand out candy. *Waaay* too much hassle. And expensive, ya know? I mean . . . *Jesus*. So we just turn out all the lights and head out for dinner while the girls trick-or-treat their way over to my sister's place on Hemlock.

I look around, all wordless, all again. Somewhere inside that Queen Anne, gentle Rain calmly folds tongues of black licorice she's lifted with a wooden spoon from a cauldron. Slow black bubbles ooze to the surface. The thick bubbles bulge, tremble, snap, and gasp.

I look at Michaela and settle on *Oh* for a response.

The candy. Maybe Claire has been using the candy for barter all this time . . .

Sylv's live dead weight presses.

Yes! Michaela says. I blink and look up at her. I had nearly forgotten she was there. And I don't even know what she's saying Yes! to.

Been doin it that way for years now, she says.

Oh, I say again, and watch her walk away, drink cup in hand. The porch-to-porch-to-porch thread of jack-o'-lanterns trembles and nods.

Jesus Christ.

I should turn out my lights, too. But I lean back on my elbows instead. It's such a beautiful night.

How many Kit-Kats and M&Ms and Snickers can a single kid eat? Is what Claire did even humanly possible? Did she even do it?

Jasmine crosses to our house to pick up Claire for trick-or-treating. She is dressed as a ladybug. She seems a little old for that, but her own personal magic allows her to pull it off just fine. Her cloud of rich brown hair pulled back into a bun and wire-rim glasses and parasol give the impression of a ladybug librarian. Adorable. I tell her sky eyes that Claire is getting ready.

She signs something. Something. And a heavy weight sinks into me again. Her hand language comes together. She's brought Halloween gifts.

She takes a seat next to me on the stoop, and places a cloth sack between her legs. She waves her arm across the span of jack-o'-lanterns topping façades across the street. Clipped shafts of lantern-light strobe through her fingers. She lowers her arm and leans her warm shoulder and head into my side. She smells of fennel, dust, and early evening dew.

I'm outta candy, I say again, and fiddle my tongue-tied hands.

She stands and signs trick-or-treat or Happy Halloween. Her eyes dance up over my shoulder at Claire, who has been sneaking up behind me, the sound of her panting amplified by the tension of the pre-chaos calm, her breath hot on the back of my neck.

"Happy Halloween!" Claire shouts. I feign surprise. Claire giggles. Jasmine and I share a look, and from her cloth sack she removes a clear glass jar with two large grasshoppers sealed inside. She extends the jar, a wiry antenna thread poking from a frayed hole pushed into the fabric of the lid.

A grasshopper leaps and slams into a clear wall and lands on its side, defeated.

Asterix! Claire squeals. Obelix! She snatches the jar from me, delighted. She presses the glass to her forehead and nose, muttering in soothing tones, teeth clenched with love.

The girls sit down and lean into me on the stoop. Jasmine reaches into her sack again. This time she removes a sandwich, wrapped in wax paper. She reaches across my chest to hand half to Claire.

Jasmine's famous and ever-present just-in-case-wich. Smells like Rain when she unwraps it. The rye bread is a century old, the slab of caraway cheddar inside a half-inch thick, topped with a sharp Hungarian mustard. It looks delicious.

The girls eat. My hunger is a cavern. Silently I wait for the burning pumpkins to tumble from porch tops to detonate the heaps of dead leaves the neighbors have carefully shaped into burial mounds on their front lawns. I struggle to remember what I couldn't taste and didn't eat over the kitchen sink less than an hour ago. The girls nod at each another and demolish the sandwich. Not a single crumb remains.

Claire wipes her mouth on her sleeve and her sleeve on her pants and runs inside to find her Q-tip shoe. Orange-and-yellow ribbons pant pink inside the jack-o'-lanterns across the street.

Jasmine's eyes twitch and I find myself drawn inside the house. Her eyes trail my every step.

Claire stands in the middle of the living room. She drops the lost-and-now-found shoe. It slaps the hardwood floor and she slips her foot inside. And all at once, her hands begin to move and I feel the tapestry of dead leaves outside rise and reconnect, as somehow it all comes together, leaf by leaf. She says she knows Mom isn't coming back. That her almost-sister will always be an almost-was.

Jasmine explained it, Claire says. It's just like her daddy. Away is gone. You have to accept that, Dad, she signs, matter of fact, You're so sad all over. All sad, she says. All over. So sad. Her hands stop. We both freeze in place, but we're not playing 'Statues.' A wad of stringy hair swells at the back of my throat. The silence of the room fills with the sound of me not vomiting.

There are four or five books stacked on one end of the bookshelf on the wall above Claire's Sylvie eyes. A vase and portrait box rest on the opposite end. There's room for an ivy or a succulent in between, but the whole thing probably works better on the other wall.

Claire's hands loop away. There's no coming back from where they went.

Her hands fall serious and silent, until she raises a goodbye palm. She drifts, and lifts her open palm again, drawn backwards across the street, through the mesh of rising and reattaching leaves, around the porch corner, and through the mist inside the older girl's cape.

Acknowledgments

Writing is hard. And a collection such as this bears a debt of profound thanks to so many, starting with those who still love me despite embodying those certain adjectives that often accompany the term *writer*.

Thank you to my readers and tellers of wise things, including but not limited to: Shannon Rutngamlug, Carmen Martines, Brad Nelson, Peter Siavelis, Ansley Kolisnyk, Manfred Gabriel, Sarah Fox, Heidi Metro, Karen Sargent, Bridget O'Meara, Molly Ramsay, and my sisters Mary Fox and Kathy Murphy and their loving families.

A very special thank you to writing coach and sanity-checker Allison Wyss. Also to editor and realist Tim Storm.

I am grateful always to my writing groups: the very crafty Black Dog Writers Jacob Wrich, Erin Lunde, Marcia Williams, and Michelle King; the Hudson literati at The Pen & Think Writers Gary Jader, Charles Ladd, Jim Guhl, Jan Dunn, Carmen Pinkerton, Anne Hollenbach, and Bev Larson.

A huge thanks, too, to fellow writers out there such as Kim Suhr at Red Oak Writing, Barry Wightman at the Wisconsin Writers Association, Daniel Pope, Courtenay Marcelo Norton, Nikki Kallio, Tom Jenks, Rick Bass, Brian Schott, Christopher Chambers, David Wanczyk, Joe Ponepinto, Kimberly King Parsons, William Burtch,

Gabe Hudson, Michael Hopkins, Kathy Fish, Amy Cipolla Barnes, Richard Mirabella, Alice Kaltman, Richard Thomas, Nickolas Butler, Robb Grindstaff, David Byron Queen, Camille Bordas, Brenda Peynado, Cheryl Pappas, Hannah Grieco, and Amber Sparks for the validation, encouragement, support, and kindness spanning the Before Times into the Now.

Sincere thank you, too, to thoughtful friend and designer Tricia Christiansen for the elegant website that allowed the crack crew at Cornerstone Press to find me. Specifically, Director and publisher Dr. Ross Tangedal, editorial director Grace Dahl, managing editor Brett Hill, and production director/cover designer Amanda Leibham. Thank you for pulling together and spinning up this beautiful book.

I will always be thankful for the lush and leafy streets that carve through the centuries-old oaks, elms, and fragrant basswoods of the town where I live, the wonderful Wisconsin weirdos everywhere, and those Sixth Street steps.

Finally, I'd like to acknowledge, with eternal gratitude, the strength and unwavering love of my wife, Stephanie, and our children Samuel, Elliot, and Leo. You kept me going, kept me grounded, kept me here.

Gratefully acknowledged are the following publications, where particular stories appeared in different forms:

Portions of "Exile" in *Wisconsin People & Ideas*

"Everyone is Dead" in *Orca, a Literary Journal*

"Larmet Lunker," "Goat Milk," and "Dumplings" in *Creative Wisconsin*

"Then It Would Be Raining" in *Whitefish Review*

"Sometimes Creek" in *New Ohio Review*

"You're Soaking in It," forthcoming in *BULL*

Several stories received citations from various publications and organizations prior to publication in this collection. Gratefully acknowledged are the following:

"Exile," First Place in the *Wisconsin People & Ideas* Fiction Contest

"Randy Koenig's Very Large Mouse," *Writer's Digest* finalist

"little blind flying mice," *Narrative Magazine* Fall Contest finalist

"Goat Milk," Jade Ring Contest Second Place, WWA

"Boydlehook," Big Sky, Small Prose finalist, *Cutbank*

"Oliebollen Destiny," *Wisconsin People & Ideas* Fiction Contest semifinalist and *Writer's Digest* Honorable Mention

"I Prefer You in Spanish," *Wisconsin People & Ideas* semifinalist

"Dumplings," Jade Ring Award Winner, WWA

"Then It Would Be Raining," Rick Bass Montana Fiction Prize Winner

"You're Soaking in It," *Writer's Digest* Honorable Mention

"Larmet Lunker," Jade Ring Second Place, WWA

STEVE FOX is the winner of the Rick Bass Montana Prize for Fiction, The Great Midwest Writing Contest, the Jade Ring Award, and a *Midwestern Gothic* Summer Flash Contest. His fiction has appeared in *New Ohio Review, Orca, a Literary Journal, Midwest Review, Midwestern Gothic, Wisconsin People & Ideas, Whitefish Review,* and others. He holds a Master of Arts in Spanish from the University of Wisconsin-Madison, and has lived and worked in four continents. Steve now resides in his home state of Wisconsin with his wife, Stephanie, three boys, and one dog.

www.stevefoxwrites.com